Turtle Dove

Six Simple Tales

Divya Dubey

GYAANA BOOKS

First published by Gyaana Books

ISBN: 978-81-909391-2-6

Gyaana Books
S-12, Plot No B-7, Street No 13, Madhu Vihar Market,
Patpadganj, Delhi 110092
www.gyaanabooks.com
(*Please contact us through our website only*)

Typeset in 11/14 Sabon

Printed and bound at Surya Print Process Pvt Ltd,
9/54, Kirti Nagar Industrial Area,
New Delhi-110015

For my parents, Sanju, and Pinku

A Note from the Author

In India, self-publishing fiction in English is still a relatively uncommon practice. At best, self-publishing is considered synonymous with the unflattering category, *vanity publishing*, an attempt by a rejected, wannabe author to aggrandise himself or herself, to make the grade as it were, simply for the satisfaction of being called a published writer.

Yet, several literary jewels have resorted to it over the centuries—Mark Twain, and several other legends included. And aren't we glad they did what they did!

Why self-publishing?

Well, why not?

If one has the requisite motivation, skills, and confidence, why not just go out there and entertain one's readers?

I had some stories to tell, and the storytelling bug in my stomach would not stop wriggling until I had done it. I wanted to do it at the earliest, and I wanted to do it my way. Hence this book. After all, the ultimate judge is the reader.

It has been an exhilarating, if a back-breaking experience, but worth every pang and muscle pull if it manages to make a mark.

I am happy that you have picked this book, and I sincerely hope you will not regret it.

Divya Dubey

Contents

Best Friend

'That's it! I've had enough. I quit!' announced Sonali, bringing both her fists down on the table with force. Her shrill voice rang plaintively, like an overused monophonic ringtone, and her uneven eyebrows knitted together in firm resolve. She continued to stare at the table, her angry fists still clenched, breathing hard.

Shailja studied her friend in silence. Sonali's hair, a long river of black silk, that she had once envied, had inexplicably and deplorably thinned during the last five years. The glistening black had discoloured and turned a jaded copper-brown. It was difficult for her to tell whether it was the work of a highlighter, or sheer malnourishment. Her hair had been brushed hard, pulled back tightly, and tied into a thin plait, which tapered down her back. Some disobedient strands lay splayed on her blouse, falling out of line with the rest.

A thick layer of bright vermilion powder in the centre parted her small head. Somehow, the striking colour in the centre emphasised the irony of her situation. As Sonali leaned back on the chair and began to drum her fingers on the table, Shailja noticed the ugly lumps of flesh she had garnered in the recent years. Her plump bulldog cheeks sagged miserably, and the second and third chins, born somewhere along the way, had been casually accepted as permanent fixtures. Who could say she was thirty-two?

Her eyes—large, bright, and neatly pencilled—were her most outstanding assets. The X-ray eyes read between the lines out of habit rather than conscious effort. She wore a pale blue and yellow sari, with zari work on it. It was draped well, as always, since she had the Virgo obsession with perfection. She had tried to train Shailja in the same art more than once, but Shailja had aborted the prodigious task soon enough. Sonali's wrists were heavily loaded with cheap glass bangles that matched her sari. There was a miniature Xerox of the Eiffel Tower, in silver, on her forehead. Dazzling earrings resembling oversized chandeliers dangled from her earlobes; and heavy, silver anklets produced a loud tinkle every time she moved a foot. Every now and again, a stray eye doused her with curious interest, but instead of being embarrassed, Sonali seemed to enjoy the attention.

Her small lips looked as though they had had three coats of crimson lipstick, outlined by a black lip liner. Every time she looked at Sonali, it made Shailja wish they had a tinted glass window separating them. The Sonali sitting before her was grossly incongruent with the image of Sonali she carried in her memory; the Sonali who had been, supposedly, her best friend for eighteen years now. In this post-marital gear and distemper make-up, Shailja decided that her friend looked very married indeed.

'He quit the job because his new boss was a woman; can you beat that? We are supposed to be living in the twenty-first century!' exclaimed Sonali. 'And that too when he'd been doing so well for himself all these months. I was beginning to hope we'd settle down at last, but no! Last time he quit his job in Kurukshetra because he didn't get along with his boss. And that was male. He said the boss had an attitude problem. It came to a showdown, and he simply stormed out. Just like that!' She snapped her fingers. 'He seems to think jobs grow on trees!'

'Hmm,' Shailja finally mumbled, feeling she ought to say *something*.

Sonali continued without a pause. 'And the time before that, when we were in Lucknow, a nice, big city like that—I had even begun to like it—he just returned from office one day and announced he'd quit. He wasn't happy with the money! Tell me, who starts a career with a six-figure salary? Five jobs in five years. Amazing!' She emphasised the last word with sullenness. 'I've had enough. I've found a flat—two bedroom—in a government colony. I'm going to shift there with my son. I've ... I've almost finalised it.' She paused reflectively. 'I'm qualified. I can get a job. Jai can stay in a crèche. I've made up my mind.'

Shailja sighed. 'It must be tough for you,' she said quietly. She had known Sonali for eighteen years. It surprised her how unencyclopaedic their knowledge of each other really was.

'Tough!' Sonali looked incredulous. 'Shail, you call it *tough*, that's it? Is that all you can say?'

'Well, you married him,' Shailja replied with a shrug.

Sonali was quiet. They were seated across each other on rickety white plastic chairs, with a white plastic table separating them, at Dilli Haat. The food stall displayed 'Momos' in bold letters on the outside. A multicoloured, old umbrella, parked at an awkward angle, shaded them inadequately from the sun—a complex, angry mass of warring Catherine Wheels in the sky at that hour. Two little children—brother and sister—raced each other somewhere in the background. A lady nearby started haggling with a shopkeeper over the price of a sleeveless cotton kurta. A young boy, from some northeastern part of the country, suddenly appeared and adjusted the pedestal fan, so that it now turned in both directions, throwing gusts of sizzling air at Sonali as well as Shailja. For a short while, it was only stranger sounds that interrupted the awkward silence. Though it was still early May, and the heat was dry, Sonali felt lumpy beads of sweat crawl, like little spiders, down her back.

'So,' she spoke at last, 'was it my fault? Was it my fault, tell me! Do you think I had any choice?'

Shailja sighed. 'We always a choice, Sonali,' she said slowly. 'We always have a choice. That is all we do have.'

Sonali looked at her like a stubborn child. She was rocking her right foot absent-mindedly, and the sound of her anklets irritated Shailja. Why were they talking about it for the fortieth time, Shailja wondered. How did she allow herself to get trapped in this futile conversation every time? She knew they would keep going round and round in circles for the next half an hour. Round and round, round and round, caught in a dizzying Merry-Go-Round. Round and round the very same issues they had been discussing and debating over forever. She had no such inclination. She felt overcome by fatigue that cleaved her bones. She suddenly had an urge to stand up and leave. How would Sonali react? Who cared! She had enough troubles of her own—troubles Sonali had no knowledge of, had never cared to enquire about.

When Shailja's mobile rang in the middle of the night, she was surprised to see Sonali's name flashing, almost urgently, on the electric-blue screen. Without any preliminaries, even though they hadn't exchanged a word in several months, Sonali declared that she wanted to see her best friend. Sonali's voice, thick with desperation, tugged at Shailja's conscience. Sonali had offered no illuminating details, no explanation. But the anxiety in her voice persuaded Shailja to agree to see her the very next day at Dilli Haat. They fixed the hour, and Shailja disconnected. And here she was as she had promised. But some essential part of her was absent. Most of Sonali's words were simply bouncing off her today. Once upon a time, she had been a sponge for her friend, absorbing everything: her bickering, her anger, her misery, her anxiety, her tears. Perhaps the sponge was saturated now. Perhaps it had suffered too much wear and tear over time.

More than genuine concern, Shailja felt it was perhaps a sense of duty that had made her agree to the meeting. The feeling of care, of legitimate concern, had evaporated aeons ago, along with all the other appurtenances of friendship that had meant so much in childhood. She wondered if that was all friendship was—a naiveté in childhood abruptly exchanged for cold detachment, and a feeble shadow of the original, in adult life. Was it just an inconsequential souvenir of a happy past? Was she growing too cynical? Had she really lost all power to feel? Some people believed love was a habit. Perhaps every emotion was. Maybe, like love, pride too was a habit. And spite. And friendship. And loyalty. Emotions were perhaps habit-forming drugs that caused narcolepsy of the soul. Maybe that was why she reacted to them mechanically, involuntarily.

Sitting across her friend, Shailja was guarded in her responses. The castles of their lives were built on either side of the Rubicon now. They had drifted, with time, into worlds divorced from each other, in directions unknown to each other. Where, once upon a time, they sought each other out to unburden their hearts of their most precious and terrible secrets, now it had become impossible to even hold a casual conversation. Small talk had never been her forte anyway, and intimacy was a stranger to them now—leaving the only possible alternative—silence.

Shailja raised her head, noticing Sonali's eyes upon her. She was chewing her lower lip with her front teeth, like a coquette contemplating her next move. Shailja raised her Cleopatra brow.

'You don't believe me, do you?' said Sonali, her voice crisp with anger.

'I didn't say that. I'm with you, of course. I think—I think it's a good decision you've taken.'

Some colour returned to Sonali's harassed face. 'Do you know what he did the other day? He was going out to the general store nearby. I told him I wanted to go along, just to get some fresh air. I have a fetish for good clothes and chic jewellery; you know that. Well, I took care to dress up. I know I didn't overdo it. Men do like their women to look good, don't they? So *I* thought. Guess what. He didn't like it one bit! He said I did that because I wanted to attract other men's attention! Can you believe that?'

Shailja sighed again. She had heard enough stories about Manish to loosely classify him as a male chauvinistic pig. He was one of those men who, during the process of evolution, had stopped at the hominid state. She was acquainted with too many of those, and knew the signs well. Manish had a ten-foot ego in his five-foot body. He found his wife's finer intellect and easy confidence unsettling. And the realisation perhaps imbruted him further, so that he would always find low, little ways to demean his wife. There was no justifiable answer to why Sonali did not retaliate.

'Did you raise an objection?' asked Shailja, even though she already knew the answer.

'Yes... of course,' Sonali's voice dropped to a guilty whisper.

'And?'

'He just waved me off. Didn't take me seriously at all! He said... he said I was being childish and immature. I was being childish and immature!' She wiped a tear from the corner of her eye.

Shailja took a sip of the fruit beer in front of her. As the northeastern boy appeared again to take the menu away, she gestured with her right hand to let it remain. He nodded, and disappeared once again. Shailja picked up the glossy menu card, rolled it, and held it up against her forehead, trying to shade her face against the unrelenting ferocity of the sun.

****

Shailja's mind flashbacked to the time they were seat partners in school. She remembered the neatly dressed, short-tempered girl who lived to laugh. Sonali was endowed with the exceptional gift of entertaining people. Her artillery of humour ranged from the grossly scatological to spontaneous bouts of incisive wit. She was a mimicry maestro, and always the first one to start the sudden, wild, uncontrollable cackle. After each act, she would burst into laughter, clapping her hands excitedly, like a five-year-old watching Tom and Jerry in action. In troubled times, people sought her out to help them forget their own problems. But Sonali always returned to Shailja, the seemingly distant, reserved classmate, who inspired more awe than friendly banter.

Once, in the Biology class, while Mrs Paasi was busy explaining the diagram of the male testis on the blackboard, amid embarrassed whispers and suppressed giggles, Sonali suddenly exclaimed, her volume turned to maximum, 'I have a *bindi* exactly like that!'

It sent all the classmates rolling on the floor, while Mrs Paasi glared at her through her large spectacles. Since Sonali had incurred her wrath, Mrs Paasi detained her after class. Sonali did what she could do best. She fainted. The doctor announced that her pulse rate was a hundred and forty a minute. Shailja had to take permission to leave early and accompany her home.

Even then, Shailja had believed that her friend was a stage-philiac. She needed to have people swarming around her, pampering her, praising her, genuflecting reverently in front of her.

'Do you know how it makes me feel?' Sonali said to Shailja once while they were walking down a corridor in school.

'What?' Shailja responded, snapping out of a reverie.

'All this false laughter, the mimicry, and the entertaining. Do you know how it makes me feel?' Sonali turned her gaze in her direction.

Shailja idly shook her head.

'It makes me feel like a performing monkey on a leash, working so that her master can eat!'

Shailja was startled to see giant tears beginning to roll down Sonali's flat cheeks. It always amazed her— Sonali's sudden, stubborn silences, and equally sudden confessions; the repeated inexplicable relapse into oceans of tears, and the ease with which she fainted in a difficult situation, like Victorian heroines. It seemed as though she could lose her blossoming consciousness, literally, at will. Sometimes, it made Shailja envy her friend's talent. It would have been such a useful tool. But in spite of her efforts, the flair for such a performance had always eluded her. She just wasn't the frail sort.

She remembered a miserable-looking Sonali turn up in school one day. After much goading she had revealed that her father insisted on taking his family to his sister's house every month. The aunt lived at the other end of town, and she loathed her with all her heart. Whenever they went visiting, the aunt would sit on a sofa during the lunch hour, looking like a juvenile spectacled cayman, with her daughters on one side, and her brother's daughter on the other, and compare them feature for feature. Her daughters were fairer, taller, better-looking. And each time, she would underline the fact, several times, driving the cudgel deeper and deeper into Sonali's heart. The fact that Sonali was brighter, that she always found a place in the top three in her class, never mattered to anybody. The ritual was repeated every time they visited.

The first time she heard about it, Shailja felt her blood would boil over, searing all her arteries and veins. She demanded to know why Sonali never raised a voice against the appalling behaviour of her aunt. Sonali shrugged.

'That's the way things work in our family.'

Shailja was aghast. She spent hours, weeks, months, trying to galvanise her dearest friend into open rebellion. She almost succeeded, once ... but not quite.

Sonali had resolved to put her jelly-foot down, and defy her father for once. This time, she promised Shailja, she would refuse to accompany her parents to her aunt's house, to be placed under the microscope and studied like bacteria. She promised she would refuse to be subjected to such outrageous humiliation.

'You wait and see, I'll do it this time!' she said, her little eyes flashing with determination.

Shailja was proud. She waited, and waited restlessly, all day to hear all about her friend's conquest. That evening, when she finally called Sonali, nobody answered the phone. The family was in Punjabi Bagh, visiting Sonali's aunt.

'Leave her alone,' Shailja's mother advised her. 'Why do you try to lead her life for her?'

'But she's my best friend!' exclaimed Shailja.

It was genuine concern then; genuine indignation. Sonali seemed to be an extension of her own self. An aspersion cast on her affected Shailja. Any finger raised at her seemed a personal affront. It made her writhe. That's what true friendship was supposed to be all about, wasn't it? She knew that Sonali needed, wanted, expected to be goaded into revealing her feelings. Any failure to do so inspired her sullenness and a frigid silence.

'Shail, just remember ... you can take the horse to the water ...' her mother began.

'I know! I know!'

Shailja deliberately turned the conversation to her new cooking classes.

A few months later, when Sonali came over to visit her, she was dressed in a lovely *malai*-cotton salwaar-kurta, exuberance emanating from her face.

'Neeru bua's here,' she said.

'Who?' For a second, it didn't register. Then Shailja said, 'The one who compares ...'

Sonali nodded excitedly. 'She got this dress for me from the US. Her son lives there. She's such a darling, isn't she? Didn't I tell you?'

'No.' Shailja was thoughtful.

'I must have forgotten,' said Sonali, squinting at her, chewing her lower lip.

'But I thought—I thought you didn't like her.'

'Oh, come on,' Sonali sniggered. 'Don't these little squabbles happen in every family?'

'Squabbles? I thought it was more than just squabbles, Sona.'

'Oh dear, I guess I carried it too far,' Sonali smiled a smile Shailja couldn't really understand. 'Must have overreacted, as usual. You know me. Come, I'll show you what else she's brought me. Come, come.'

Shailja had wondered then if her mother was right. Was she investing too much of herself in their friendship? Was she fiercely battling for a non-existent cause? Little particles of doubt left little abrasions in her heart.

A few years later, however, when the girls crossed the sheltered life of school and entered college, Shailja's hopes resurfaced. Their friendship had survived, if barely, through the vagaries of the weather, through the temperamental tides. Shailja was still hopeful. They had had enough debates and discussions, had graduated from dissecting rats to dissecting Nietzsche and Sartre, together. They had spent more than a few taxing evenings discussing things that really mattered. In spite of their divergent paths (now that Shailja had opted for English in a different college, while Sonali had enrolled for the Sciences), if they sincerely made an attempt, they could still find a genuine common ground to hold them together.

'The other day,' Sonali told her, 'I did it. I held my ground.'

'What happened?'

'There was this salwaar-kurta—a brilliant orange one with large print on it. I really liked it though my mother didn't. We had to go for a birthday party—my niece's. Mummy wouldn't allow me to wear it. She said it made me look even darker. But I insisted upon wearing it. It was a full-fledged quarrel! Both of us were fuming. She didn't speak to me all evening. Renu mausi commented on my dress too, but I didn't react. It was such a little thing ... and they made such a mountain out of it!'

Shailja smiled. In spite of herself, she was glad. True, orange didn't suit Sonali much ... but hey, what the hell!

****

More people walked into Dilli Haat: couples, pairs and trios of college friends; small, scattered groups of curious tourists. The tables around them were slowly filling up.

'I wouldn't have been me had it not been for you,' said Sonali, running her forefinger over an eyebrow. Her bangles glittered in the sunlight.

'That's not true,' replied Shailja. 'Each man makes himself. I can't say I did anything earth-shaking for you.'

'You've influenced me a lot,' Sonali insisted. 'More than you know.'

Shailja shrugged. 'Well, we're all influenced by the company we keep,' she returned with a light smile.

'No, not like that. I meant ... something different. I didn't realise how much I had imbibed from you. All these years as—as a married woman—your words kept coming back to me all the time ... under different circumstances.'

'Aha.'

Though Sonali's words seemed indubitably sincere, Shailja remained unmoved. At a more sanguine time, they might have flattered her, but now, she swept them away like gossamers. She asked herself the same string of rhetorical questions she asked every time. Just why did everything Sonali say and do feel like vacuum now? Why did her words flip over her ears without making any impression, leave alone a lasting one? Mighty waves of past images crashed against the rocks of her mind. She found them lapping away the sands of sensation and sentiment yet again.

****

Shailja remembered a time during university days when, while returning from college, they had met on a Blueline bus. It had been a long day for her, one of those when-nothing-goes-right ones. Shailja had had a marathon session on Shakespeare in class. She still had to write an assignment on Lady Macbeth. The bus was even more overcrowded than usual. As she climbed in, she spotted Sonali, wildly flailing her arms to attract her attention. She waved back. It was, as always, a gruelling task to make her way to her friend in that filthy swarm. Her nostrils cringed as she wrestled past smelly armpits and moist moustaches.

Stops came and went. Shoes tip-tapped, squeaked and squelched, but nobody seemed to get off the bus. The dank human bodies were still stuck together like stubborn price labels on gift items. Getting unstuck brought the same feeling—of being rudely ripped apart. Shailja and Sonali stood near the rear end, one hand slippery with sweat, holding onto the squeaky metal rod over their heads; the other clutching their bags. Elbows and knees jostled, pushed, and shoved, indiscriminately. In the claustrophobic jungle of human heads, Shailja desperately gasped for breath. When at last they reached ITO, the bus disgorged a sea of people at the roadside. It was miraculous, the number of humans a little Blueline packed into it every day. Now that the crowd had thinned inside, Shailja and Sonali stretched their atrophied legs and moved closer, allowing themselves to breathe.

'You know,' Sonali turned to face her suddenly. 'You remember Ghazal, the pretty girl you were so friendly with back in class twelve?'

'Yes,' Shailja replied, trying to maintain her balance. Her legs were still sore. 'Still am.'

Shailja wondered why Sonali had suddenly remembered that awkward phase of their lives. It had become impossible to communicate or connect with Sonali during that time. Initially, she had borne it with patience. She would answer her prying questions with good humour and satisfy her curiosity. She would tell her where she was going and who she was meeting. Later, it began to rattle her nerves. She wasn't married to Sonali. Why was Sonali behaving like a miserable, nagging wife? The situation kept going from bad to worse without any accounting for it until, ultimately, Shailja distanced herself from her best friend for a few months. She refused to meet or speak to her.

Though they eventually got over the crisis, Shailja never mentioned that period. That phase was still foggy, still puzzling. It still unnerved her when she thought about it.

'I hated you then,' Sonali said softly. She looked at Shailja, as if staring through smoked glass. The inscrutable look had returned. She was chewing her lower lip. 'I hated you. I hated it more than anything. It was impossible to bear. Even when I joined college, for a month initially, I went around telling all my friends that you were a bitch!'

Shailja stared at her, mute with wonder. A year had elapsed since they had left school. Shailja still didn't like to speak about that dreadful period. She had asked Sonali no questions during those mystifying days, never demanded any explanations. It was perhaps the best thing in the circumstances. For months she had left her phone ringing frantically through the day (or night), firmly refusing to answer it. She had maintained silence when she could not evade her friend. She had borne her relentless temper tantrums with quiet dignity. She had endured her severe lashings, and nursed her injuries, without complaint.

'Thanks a lot,' she said at last, sarcastically.

Sonali's uneven teeth flashed a delighted smile, and she cackled again—the same, sudden, wild cackle Shailja recognised well. She offered no further elucidating details, and no apology. Shailja wondered what had inspired this sudden confession. She had made friends with Ghazal in class eleven, when they chose the same subjects together. Ghazal was a lovely girl, and they had hit it off together like toast and omelette instantly. She had always known that Sonali tended to be a tad—well—resentful, but then there had appeared a strange void between them. Despite her best efforts, it had rapidly acquired canyonic proportions. She could do nothing to check the damage. Sonali wouldn't allow her to. And then she gave up the effort altogether. There were some things only time could fix, if they could be fixed at all.

'Do you remember the day you came to see me, and wouldn't stop crying?' said Shailja.

Sonali nodded.

'I kept asking you what had happened, and you wouldn't tell me.'

Sonali nodded again.

'I tried to be a friend to you, you know. I really did,' Shailja was sincere.

Sonali offered no comment.

'I—I didn't know where I stood with you. One moment we'd be best friends, and the next moment you'd behave as if you didn't recognise me!'

'That's not true.'

'Then tell me why you never told me what was bothering you so much. Something was. I know it. Didn't you trust me?'

'Of course I did,' Sonali replied, biting her lip. 'You know I did.'

'Then why didn't you ever just speak to me? You became quite ... peculiar after that!'

Sonali shrugged.

'Well, will you tell me now?' Shailja ventured again. 'It's been a mystery to me for more than a year.'

'I can't.'

Sonali turned away brusquely, and started staring out of the rusty, broken Blueline window.

****

Confused, ghostly voices in the distance.

'Rukun bhai, it's your daughter's malefic *saaya* upon your business. Hopeless situation. Nothing can be done. It's your destiny. No amount of pujas or rituals can help you now.'

Her father's frowning face. Shaking heads.

'No solution ... tch tch ... no solution at all! You've lost money, of course. I can see that. I know you have been going through a great deal. Hmm, you'll lose more in the days to come. Yes, yes, I can guarantee it. Your business will not survive, that's plain.

Her mother's troubled eyes.

'Yes, yes, bhai saab, I have performed the most powerful pujas for you, you know that ... Okay ... hmph ... I'll try something else this time.'

Whispers. Whispers. Whispers.

'What? No respite? *He bhagwaan*! The planetary positions are really malevolent. She's blight upon the family's fortunes, that girl! No shame! That child was born at a terrible hour.'

Eyes staring at her from all directions: accusing, resigned, curious.

'Let me study her birth chart again. What can be done ... hmm ... let me think. It's a catastrophe ... tch, tch. This girl ... trust me, she'll bring ruin upon you if you are not careful.'

More dirty looks.

'All right ... all right. If you have *so much* faith in us, we'll have to think of a solution, isn't it? *Just* for your sake, Rukun bhai. It'll take you a lot of effort, and firm resolve, but you'll have to take the right steps, bhai saab. It is the only solution, you understand, no, bhai saab?'

Honeyed tones. Soothing voices.

'Think about it, Rukun bhai. It's the only way out for the whole family. It's your wish. Otherwise, doom is certain.'

Closed doors. Decibels rising and falling. Silence.

'What? You'll do it? Good, good. You're a wise man, Rukun bhai. It will cleanse the soul, I promise.'

A strong smell of incense.

A faint sound of rhythmic chanting.

Mud-coloured walls of a mouldy room, infested with tiny insects staring back brazenly at her.

Why did her head seem so woozy? Sleepy. She felt very sleepy.

A familiar masculine scent. Where had she smelt the musk before? She knew it well, didn't she? At home. Yes, at home. She smelt it every morning, didn't she?

The soft sound of a zip unzipped.

And then, thick blue-grey veins suddenly glaring derisively from ugly, large hands—the hands she knew so well—pushing her skirt up her thighs slowly, surely.

And then, *a snaky, searing piece of flesh pushing deep and hard, tearing the bare insides of her labia, moving up and down, up and down—again and again, again and again, again and again* ....

****

The momos arrived on two separate plates, vegetarian, and non-vegetarian—ivory coloured triangles, soft, steamed, and delicious. Sonali poured some hot chutney over her non-meaty ones.

Once again Shailja questioned her own motive for being present there today. What did she expect to give, or gain? Wasn't she tired of the circularity of time and event in her life? What was she trying to seek? She knew their relationship had replicated the peaks and troughs of an ECG ribbon, through the long years. Had the peaks and troughs fused into a long, level beep-beep of a lifeless heart? Is that why she had come now—to confirm her nagging suspicions?

'Was it late when I called last night?' asked Sonali.

'No, not really,' Shailja replied after a second. 'I hadn't fallen asleep. It was only a few minutes past twelve.'

****

Shailja turned the leaves of her memory randomly, pausing at certain dog-eared pages that marked the more significant events. She recalled the last time her phone had rung in the middle of the night. It was half a decade ago. Once again, without any preliminaries, words had gushed out of Sonali's mouth like water through a village tube well.

'I want to see you! Kunal is sick!' she had choked over the phone. 'Suicide attempt!'

She had started crying. The rest of the words were incoherent. Shailja had to soothe her before she could proceed.

'He's consumed rat poison! Come quickly! Oh, I don't know what we'll do!'

She began howling again. The sobs were noisy enough to make Shailja squirm.

She had woken her mother, a gynaecologist, who ran her own clinic. Together they had rushed to Sonali's house, ten kilometres away. Though the night was thick and cold, both of them felt tired and warm. As they entered, they found Sonali's mother on the floor, her blank face splotched with tears. Household items lay scattered on the floor, like contorted bodies after a riot. The furniture lay covered with multiple layers of grime. Dust-sodden cobwebs shrouded the drapery. Everything everywhere spoke of gross neglect.

Their entry had not been noticed. Sonali was strangely quiet. Together, Shailja and her mother physically lifted the young boy, Sonali's brother, from the bed, and carried him to the car. There were no brawny male members to offer help. The two friends who had been with him had run for a doctor in panic, and had not returned. Shailja's mother quickly rang some contacts and arranged for his hospitalisation.

It wasn't a suicide attempt, a dazed, much frightened friend of Kunal's informed Shailja later. He was overwrought, repeating the story to hoards of people again and again, like a twenty-four-hour news channel. Kunal had called some friends over for dinner. They had been watching cricket. In his excitement, he had mistaken the rat poison bottle for his cough syrup. He hadn't checked the label.

While Shailja listened to the story, Sonali sat sulkily in a corner, her pretty eyes unfocused. They were rivers of fierce emotion, flooding her face, the landscape of her cheeks, giving her a corpselike appearance. Her mother had decided to stay home which, they thought, was sensible. While Shailja's mother rushed to and fro, making arrangements, and signing different forms, bouts of hysteria afflicted Sonali. She would burst into tears and whimper, a flurry of accusations escaping her lips every few minutes. It was punctuated by moments of perfect lucidity whenever required.

'Stop it, SONALI!' Shailja bellowed at last.

'My brother, my brother!' Sonali cried hoarsely, making the situation more theatrical than it was.

'Kunal's all right! Nothing will happen. Calm down! It was an *accident*. It was an *accident*, all right? He's stable now. It's okay!'

The charade lasted a couple of hours. Shailja's taut spine felt crippled with pain. Each tired bone howled for rest. There was no extra bed, no kapok mattress she could rest on for a while. She felt appalled at her friend's frenzied behaviour. Yet, she could not afford to lose her temper right now. Somebody had to remain sane.

'He's not okay! He'll die!' Sonali sobbed again. 'Why don't you understand!'

'SONALI! STOP IT RIGHT NOW, I SAY!' Shailja screamed.

She had been trying long, and trying hard. But there was a limit to human endurance. A very weary Shailja had just crossed it. The next few seconds evaporated as fast as acetone. Her strong, wrathful arm swung and struck Sonali's left cheek hard. It was a tight, unpremeditated slap.

The unexpected blow cured Sonali of her hysteria. But it left Shailja trembling, and disturbed. She slipped into the chair before her. Exhaustion—physical and mental, lack of sleep, and acute tension burst upon her shoulders and seeped into every muscle. She experienced fear, a thing she was absolutely unused to. And along with fear, she found the double helix—of disgust and contempt—stealthily and steadily uncoiling inside. For those few moments, her heart was a gallimaufry of undisciplined emotions.

She stared at the wild-eyed creature in front of her. Could it be the same Sonali she had known all her life? It was ... the same Sonali who had spent a lifetime with her, sticking with her through her darkest days as she waddled through the Loch Ness of her troubles; the same Sonali who had compromised her own study hours to help her plod through Chemistry before exams; the same Sonali who had taken charge when she broke up with Raj, in the middle of her MA first year final exams—when her own brain seemed to have gone bust. It was the same woman who had broken all records in school by scoring a hundred per cent in History in her class ten finals; the Sonali who had had an aeroplane contrail of awards to her name, and a promising career ahead. It was the same woman, who, when her father died suddenly one day after his business collapsed, had taken life by the scruff of its neck and turned it around once more.

Shailja and her mother spent the night at the hospital. They left in the morning, Shailja dragging her stiff legs to the car, in complete silence. A brush with her friend's unnerving histrionics, the theatricality of the act, had unsettled her. As she left, Sonali waved. Shailja waved back. Sonali's eyes, at once piercing and squinting, disconcerted her.

That day, Shailja had a disturbed sleep, her subconscious mind traversing gradients of black. Shadows of random, disconnected episodes fogged her mind. And from the dense fog, only one figure emerged—her best friend. She saw her cackling, squinting, laughing at her. She woke to see the same eyes greet hers now. Sonali had been sitting in her room for a quarter of an hour, waiting for her to wake up.

'I am sorry,' she said at last. 'For—for my behaviour in hospital. I don't know what I'd have done without you!'

Apologies poured forth from Sonali's lips. They sat there talking for four long hours. They bared their hearts to each other once again, waiting for the nimbus to break.

They parted at last with promises of eternal friendship, loyalty, and faith.

A week later, while she was waiting for the bus, a red Maruti Suzuki braked and stopped beside Shailja. She was surprised to see Sonali's face as the window rolled down.

'Come, get in,' said Sonali, obviously pleased to see her.

Shailja obeyed. Neither mentioned the episode that had occurred the week before. As for Sonali, she seemed to have no recollection of it at all. Her laughter was back, and she chattered incessantly.

'Going to the book fair tomorrow?' Shailja asked her after a while.

'Yes, of course.'

'Good. I'll wait at the bus stop, and hop into the bus when I see you. Just wave as usual, will you?'

'No need; I'll pick you up.'

'Oh! You have this car at your disposal, do you?' said Shailja, looking around. 'Lucky girl! Whose car is it by the way? Looks new.'

'Why, ours of course!'

'Yours? What do you mean?'

'We bought it. It came a week ago. Didn't I tell you?'

'No.'

Shailja felt confused and hurt that her friend should have excluded her from the little good news just after the pledges they had taken the week before.

'Oh, how strange!' said Sonali, squinting again. 'I thought I did.'

****

The boy from the northeast appeared again. Shailja had an irrational urge to call out to him. But she checked herself and gestured instead. He came over to the table. Did they want anything else? Shailja looked at Sonali. Sonali shrugged.

'Okay, another fruit beer then.'

'And some hakka noodles?'

'Two glasses of fruit beer, and a plate of hakka noodles, please,' she ordered.

The boy nodded and went away. The smell of freshly cooked *thukpa* wafted from the kitchen. It was pleasing to Shailja's nostrils. She lifted herself and readjusted the umbrella. The sun had travelled a few paces, leaving a part of their table in the shade. Its glowering face had become milder; the fury assuaged after trudging tiredly through the day.

Shailja waited for a while, contemplating her next question. Her fingers idly played with the salt bottle on the table.

'Would it have been different had you married Jatin?' she asked hesitantly.

Sonali stopped shaking her foot. She looked up, straight into Shailja's honest eyes. 'I knew you would ask me this question someday. Even the day I got married, I knew it would come. I've been waiting all these years.'

Her smile was wreathed in sorrow.

'Tell me,' Shailja waited.

'Well, maybe... and maybe not,' she replied after a minute, her face laminated with prelapsarian innocence. 'After all, how well did I know him?'

'*Well*!'

'Well, all right... there was a little involvement for a while... but those things are so *transient*, especially when you are young.'

'Do you really feel like that?'

'Yes.'

'And you've never felt any different... all these years?'

'No.'

'Are you quite sure?'

'Yes. I love Manish.'

'Maybe Jai has more to do with it.'

Pause. 'Maybe. How does it matter? I'm a married woman.'

'I know,' said Shailja, looking at her. 'I know.'

Amongst all the bookmarked pages in Shailja's memory, this was where the red satin ribbon was firmly placed.

Sonali's employment as an adhoc lecturer in Delhi had brought her into contact with Jatin. He was a young colleague, already renowned for his early academic lustre amongst the university elite. He was short, fair, and unhandsome. She was tall, dark, and lovely. It wasn't love at first sight. Nor the second, third, fourth or fifth. In fact, neither realised when they succumbed to the charming tribulations of love—insane and intense. But Sonali thought it must have been during one of the university seminars.

He was a true romantic—wangling hours from packed schedules for cups of the four-rupee coffee they shared at relatively deserted university canteens. His mischievous light grey eyes laughed even when speaking about serious matters. He was enamoured with her scintillating remarks, and her brilliantly articulate observations about the most mundane things. He was one of the few who understood her. Her coquetry robbed him of self-possession. She was a rhapsodic verse of poetry, a lyrical masterpiece in motion. She was drunk with the staggering power of his passion. For those few months, she was ecstasy's own daughter.

'He thinks I'm beautiful!' she exclaimed, clapping her hands like child, the minute she met Shailja.

In the days that followed, she arrived and left suddenly, unexpectedly, always bringing some nuggets of his wisdom to share with Shailja—some anecdote, some secret treasure he had bestowed upon her. She informed her that he belonged to a modern, easygoing family. They were not fastidious. They were model, modern-day parents, and would welcome any alliance as long as their son's happiness was ensured.

'He said I'm delicious,' she announced once, joy spilling from her drunken eyes. 'D-e-l-i-c-i-o-u-s. Can you believe it!'

Shailja smiled. She was glad for her friend.

Life does not serve victories on a silver platter, little or large. Sonali soon discovered that she had a rival. Jyotika was Jatin's buxom, apple-cheeked friend who had known him for over two years. She had chosen him as the object of her overt affections. She wore platforms and drank Jack Daniel's. She was bosom pals with all the vices Sonali envied and admired. The contrast was even starker when the two women stood together. To top it all, she had taken a firm dislike to Sonali from day one. When Jatin announced to her that he was in love with her and not Jyotika, she had kissed him.

'He chose me! Ha, one joy scatters a hundred griefs!' she said again and again, dancing around Shailja. 'Do you know how it feels to be the chosen one?'

A few days later, Sonali informed Shailja that Jatin was in a dilemma. He had an offer from a well-known university in Vancouver. Scholarship was a certainty. If Fortuna winked in his direction, he could be on his way to realising the dream of a lifetime. He would be a research scientist.

'So what do you plan to do?' asked Shailja.

'He—he's asked me to marry him!'

'Really? Wow!'

Shailja hugged her. It was a warm, friendly hug, reserved for the rarest occasions and the most special people. Display of emotion wasn't Shailja's forte either.

Jatin and Sonali got engaged at Sonali's house. Shades of silver adorned Sonali's sequined sari, and complemented Jatin's silk sherwani. The ceremony was attended by their immediate family and closest friends. Lakshmi and Ganesh united to bless the occasion. Sonali was on cloud nine—nay—ten. In those merry hours, she tasted the sugar and sauce of life. She pranced and pirouetted, her cackle ringing throughout the house.

Nobody knew what happened... or why. Ten days after the ceremony, Sonali called Shailja, frantic and distraught.

'I *have* to see you. Immediately!'

'What happened? Everything all right?'

'Nothing is all right!' Sonali howled.

Sonali's tau ji, her father's elder cousin, who had not been a part of the engagement ceremony, had taken great offence. He was the eldest amongst all her uncles.

Nobody could discount his opinion while taking a serious decision. He had already decided upon another family of his acquaintance for Sonali's marriage. He had had her in mind for sometime now. And being an elder of the family, he had, of course, believed it to be his own responsibility. He had spoken to the boy of his choice. He was now pressing her only parent to renege on her promise to Jatin, warning her of dire consequences if she refused. Sonali's mother had already begun to sway under pressure. None of the other relatives dared to intervene.

They sat upstairs in Shailja's little L-shaped bedroom, pondering over the sticky situation.

'I don't believe this,' said Shailja, shaking her head. 'They can't do this. How can they do this when you are already engaged?'

'Engaged, but not married yet.'

'Even then … Sona, you love him, don't you?'

'What a thing to ask! Of course!'

'Then, will you allow them to get away with this?'

'No way!' Sonali's sharp eyes kindled with firm resolve again. 'No way! It's the question of my life.'

'Think about it. Don't let yourself down. At least, think of Jatin. You can't forsake him, can you? He adores you. He'll be devastated if you dither now.'

'I know! It's different this time. I know he's counting on me.'

'Well then, we are with you. If you want to go ahead and marry, we'll do all we can to help. You can count on us.'

'Thanks so much! All this is so ridiculous!'

'You have to fight it out this time, Sona.'

'I will.' said Sonali firmly. 'Believe me, I will!'

Shailja raised her voice against the injustice too. She cried herself hoarse—until she realised that hers was the only voice railing against the act. There was no accompanying voice. Sonali had disappeared. Shailja remembered Jatin's frantic calls to her the following week, and the weeks after. She still remembered his pleading, traumatised voice. She could feel his anguish and bewilderment. She saw the cinders of emotion abruptly crackle and dwindle within him. But she was helpless to help him. Sonali had disappeared without a word to her. She had left no clue about her whereabouts. The feeling of betrayal haunted her as much as it haunted Jatin.

The phone calls continued for three months. Jatin called every alternate day. He had tried Sonali's residence and been rebuffed. He had tried her relatives—the ones he knew—but they had turned away from him, or had turned him away. He'd gone from one house to the next, defeated and distressed. He visited Shailja again, but she found it impossible to face him even though she knew she was guiltless. There was too much anguish in those eyes; and somewhere, somehow, she felt she had failed her friend.

In the fourth month, Sonali resurfaced. Derangement was written all over her face. She looked like a crumbling mass of ancient papyrus. She appeared on a quiet afternoon, just when Shailja was planning to take a nap. She knocked the door, ambled in, and ensconced herself in the little hollow at the corner of Shailja's bed, her favourite seat. Shailja asked no questions. Sonali offered no explanations. A stream of tears flowed down her sallow cheeks for half an hour.

'I did it for my mother,' she whispered finally, her trembling hand wiping her eyes. 'I did it for my mother...'

Shailja stared at her suffering eyes.

'Say I did the right thing!' she said, shaking Shailja's shoulders. Her eyes were wild; her voice, desperate. 'Say I did the right thing!'

Shailja was surprised at the vehemence in her voice. *Real friendship does not freeze in winter*, Shailja remembered. Sonali pleaded guilty. She had collapsed under pressure. She admitted that she had not had the strength to fight her own battles. Again and again Shailja heard the same refrain, 'I did it for my mother.'

The feeling of scorn, disdain, and nausea swelled inside Shailja every time she heard Sonali speak. Emotion argued against reason. Loyalty demanded a flagrant disregard for justice. But somehow, she could not bring herself to condone her dearest friend this time. Jatin's distraught face lingered in her memory, stubbornly.

'Come on, say I did the right thing,' Sonali pleaded again, her long fingernails clamped onto Shailja's shoulders, pressing them till they hurt.

'I have nothing to say,' Shailja blurted out at last.

It was six months before they could resume normal conversation, or salvage whatever they could of their shipwrecked relationship. Would it have been easier to forgive her if Sonali's plea had been devoid of the cataphasic refrain, 'I did it for my mother'? Shailja couldn't say. She hated herself for being judgemental, but it was beyond her power to desist. It was as though by chanting those words again and again, Sonali had surrendered the only means of redemption available to her.

It was through a common friend that she learnt Sonali had recently accepted a man one of their family friends had recommended to her. Shailja had been unaware of the developments. Though not blatantly ostracised, she felt she had become an insignificant, peripheral item in Sonali's life.

She congratulated Sonali on the phone.

'I didn't know you had said yes.'

'Really? That's impossible! How could you not have known? I told everybody!'

Shailja said nothing.

'But you have to be there at the wedding, of course!' Sonali added immediately. 'Can't get married without you there! You are a family member. You must help me with everything.'

Shailja saw Manish once—on the wedding day. And whatever she did get a glimpse of left her unimpressed. She had not anticipated the scale of the wedding—the magnificence, the pomp, the flamboyance. There was a cinemascope display of colour and pyrotechnics. The filigree dazzled her. Every facet of the wedding was a glaring assertion of the reality of the event. Perhaps Shailja was still in denial that everything seemed surreal to her.

'Come, come, see my *lehenga*,' Sonali's cheerful face materialised beside her, taking her hand, and leading her into the antechamber in excitement. 'It weighs twelve kilos, you know!'

Dumbly Shailja followed her. She looked at the bride. There was no hint of guilt, no trace of regret, no memory of the event that had left such a deep cicatrix on Shailja's own life. Suddenly, she found the music too loud, the room too claustrophobic. The blood-red *lehenga* with its goldthread embroidery clashed against the series of pictures running amok in her mind. She couldn't bear to stay at the wedding she had once believed she would never want to miss.

And that was the picture of Sonali's wedding—Sonali displaying the twelve-kilo, blood-red *lehenga*—that her memory had kept forever framed.

Shailja completed her Masters in Literature from Calcutta and returned to Delhi to work. Sonali was more than thrilled when Shailja announced her engagement to David, a colleague at her workplace. Sonali congratulated her with warm hugs. She joyfully added that she looked forward to dancing at Shailja's wedding. Shailja felt her absence the most the day she got married.

****

Shailja checked her watch. It was half past four. She had to leave soon.

'He married Jyotika, you know,' said Sonali complainingly, shaking her right foot again.

Shailja looked at her. Sonali's eyes did not flicker.

'Jatin—he married Jyotika—that bitch! How could he do that to me!'

'Do that to *you*?' Shailja was amazed. 'You have the gall to say that, Sona, after what you did to him?'

'Well, he forgot me, didn't he? He forgot me anyway. He moved on.'

'What else was he supposed to do? Can you blame him?' Shailja almost snapped. This was impossible!

Sonali wouldn't answer.

Shailja shook her head and glanced at her watch again.

'You have to leave now, do you?' Sonali asked her tentatively, downing the remnants of her third glass of fruit beer.

'Yeah… I… need to go to the hospital.'

'What happened?'

'Oh, just a check up. The gynaecologist wants to take a look at my system. It's been sometime since the marriage…'

Sonali nodded, comprehending her. There was an embarrassed silence.

'Let me know whatever happens,' said Sonali.

'I will, and you too. I think it's a good idea you've come up with. It'll give you independence, and some time to think things over.'

'I will, certainly.' Sonali pushed the rickety chair back, and picked up her tawdry blue purse. 'Take care.'

Both of them knew there would be no call. Shailja waved as Sonali's car left.

Months later, she tried Sonali on her old mobile number. Surprisingly, there was a ring and a reply. They chatted.

'I'm expecting,' Shailja told her after a while. 'At last.'

Sonali squealed with genuine joy. 'Congratulations! I am so happy for you!'

'Thanks. What about you? How are you? How have things been?'

'Oh… I told you Manish quit his last job, right? But he found another one… He's a senior manager now… Yes, yes, we'll be staying on in Delhi… No, no, I'm not moving out after all…It wouldn't have worked, you know. Manish can't manage without me, as you know. Yes, yes, we'll be shifting to Dwarka, that's all. Didn't I tell you? I thought I did…'

Shailja lifted her head and stared as the first drops of rain kissed the emerald leaves of the mango tree outside the window. She thought of Sonali and herself eighteen years ago, sharing private jokes, giggling over Linda Goodman, and devouring her mother's special *lifafa paratha*s on the garden swing, in the brilliant loaming on a summer day.

Arnab

Had it not been for Protima *mashi*, I may not have been born at all. She strolled into the building that day, clad in a Bengali cotton sari, tailing her husband and four other helpers, as they moved into their new flat. Ours was one of those not very upmarket colonies in east Delhi. She sat down on an old suitcase, while the men unloaded the luggage from the brown truck spattered with ditch water.

Several pairs of eyes played Peeping Tom from the neighbouring houses. Some peeked from half-open doors near the landing; some smiled, unabashed, from their little balconies. Mr Roy addressed the workers, groping for suitable Hindi equivalents for seemingly untranslatable Bengali words. Sometimes he found them, while some comments caused his audience to crack up immediately. But he just smiled benignly at everybody.

His wife was at least twenty years younger. She couldn't have been much younger than my mother really, but her baby frame topped with a baby face highlighted the contrast between them. She looked on disinterestedly as the luggage was taken down and carried into their new flat. In the end, she took it upon herself to carry the last item—a little leather briefcase—upstairs. She had to use both her hands to lift it. At our landing, she paused to snatch some oxygen from the torrid air. My mother opened her door wide and stepped outside to greet her new neighbour. In return, 'Mrs Roy' gave her a brilliant smile.

My mother invited her in. Mrs Roy (Protima *mashi* as I came to call her later) declined the invitation, pleading exhaustion, but promised her that she would see her very soon. However, as my mother began to retrace her steps into the house, she slipped and almost succumbed to what might have been a fatal fall. If someone rescued her from the menacing jaws of miscarriage at that point, it was Protima *mashi*. In a flash, she had abandoned her luggage and appeared at my mother's side, saving her life, and in turn my own.

She couldn't have been more compassionate with her own kith and kin. But then, had it been her own kith and kin, she would have probably turned a blind eye upon them. She tended to the perfect stranger for days, unmindful of her own delicate condition. I don't know if she was aspiring to become Florence Nightingale II, but she did attempt a thorough imitation. It was perhaps an instant, unspoken bond formed between two ladies sailing on the same ship at the same time. But their concurrent pregnancy was certainly responsible for the spontaneous bond they established.

My mother discovered that Protima *mashi* had a highly elastic tongue and, once she had found it, it would not stop waggling. Mother also found that not only did Protima *mashi* look like a child, she was one. Everybody and everything interested her—no matter how trivial. Everybody and everything worried her as well. She would clasp any stray remark to her heart and brood over it for days, letting her tongue wiggle-waggle until it had completed the post mortem. She treated her neighbours' problems with a sense of proprietorship, and worried about them more than they did. Nobody knew whether it was them or herself she was constantly trying to soothe with her reassuring words. Prattling was a birthright.

The children of the neighbourhood considered her a comrade, and treated her like one. She could instinctively understand and speak their language. She played all indoor games with them, and cheated overtly at carom or Scrabble. Like any good player, she always disowned defeat, and steered clear of any responsibility for it. Sometimes, the kids would deliberately pull her leg until she became piqued, or flew into a blistering rage. Then they would snigger, and nudge her till she too began to laugh. In fact, it was through the little monkey brigade in the society that the entire neighbourhood came to know her.

Protima *mashi* had one ardent desire. She desperately wanted her child to be a daughter. She prayed frantically for a daughter. She was glowing in her sixth month, she had turned fairer, she was regularly experiencing her morning and evening sickness, and she was craving for all the right things; whereas my mother, even at the end of her last trimester, was neither glowing, nor craving for eats—of any kind. She wasn't fussing about her morning or evening sickness either. *Mashi* would spend hours discussing all her new developments with my patient and uncomplaining mother, and all the other assortment of housewives in the building.

One afternoon, she turned up at our door, perceptibly very excited. The XXL-size red *bindi* on her little forehead, her most prominent identifying feature, popped up and down as she looked at my mother.

'*Didi! Jaanish ki holo*?' she said to my non-Bengali mother. *Sister, do you know what happened*?

My mother continued kneading the dough, smiling. '*Na re*. How will I know anything sitting inside this little pigeonhole? Tell me.'

Protima *mashi* playfully waved the knotted end of her pallu at my mother and laughed shyly.

'Didi, we went to my mother's this weekend, you know that, don't you?' she said, taking her place near my mother on the floor.

'Of course.'

'Now, *ma* has this friend ... well, sort of *ma*'s *boudi*—an elderly lady. She's a seer ... a kind of astrologer, you know.'

'I see,' said my mother, suddenly interested.

'She tells people all kinds of things. I told *ma* I would like to see her, and guess what? She is coming down to visit us on Saturday!'

'What!'

'*Sotti*!' said Protima *mashi*, nodding vigorously. 'She is coming down to our house, right here in two days' time. She'll be able to tell us all we want to know. I want you to be there.'

'Of course!' said my mother, turning out perfectly round little *puris* from the spattering oil in the wok. 'I will not miss it for anything!'

It was a small ceremony in their little flat. The list of invitees included only our family. Mother was more of a co-hostess, so I guess my father was the only genuine guest. He and Mr Roy enjoyed their drinks and snacks stealthily in Mr Roy's little study, and pulled their wives' legs, as the ladies continued making their arrangements. *Mashi* and my mother spent the morning sweeping the block-tile floor, dusting the sparse furniture, laying fresh cotton carpets on the ground, and preparing a splendid meal. The much awaited guest of honour finally arrived, dressed in a saffron cotton cloth; and Kolhapuris, which she took off at the doorstep. She was indeed very old, in her nineties perhaps. She ensconced herself quietly on the little mat on a little *peedi* mashi had positioned especially for her near the *pujor ghor*.

She began the ritual almost right away, without any accompanying footnotes, leaving the men staring at each other, bamboozled. She spent some time in perfect silence, mumbling some abstruse words to herself. She was oblivious to the bewildered humans around her staring expectantly at her lined face. From the little soiled bundle she carried with herself, she brought out a tiny gold ring. She asked *mashi* for a long piece of thread. *Mashi* briefly left her spot on the carpet, and soon reappeared with a spool of black thread from her bedroom. She handed it politely to the nonagenarian who pulled a long string and snapped it free easily even with her false teeth. She slung the thread through the slim circle of gold, and tied the loose ends together, so that the ring hung from one end now.

Surprisingly, she called my mother to her first. My mother looked at Protima *mashi* tentatively. Somewhat reassured by her encouraging smile, she walked over to the elderly lady and sat down in front of her. The lady asked her to put the closed fist of her right hand forward. Mother obliged. The lady held up the double thread over her wrist, with the golden ring dangling from it, and closed her eyes. She seemed to be reading a mantra in her mind. Almost miraculously, the thread began to oscillate over mother's wrist. Left to right, right to left it swung as if of its own volition.

'Aha,' the lady spoke, smiling. 'Thou shalt have a son, woman.'

My mother thanked her awkwardly, and retreated with a courteous bow. Next, the old lady called Protima *mashi* forward. *Mashi* scampered to her excitedly. The lady asked her to put her fist forward too, and repeated the ritual. All inquisitive eyes turned towards the dangling gold ring with keen expectation. Immediately, the ring began to move, sketching concentric circles over Protima *mashi*'s wrist.

The lady smiled again. 'For you a daughter, my daughter,' she said.

To say that Protima *mashi* was drunk with delight over the next few weeks, would be an understatement. My mother went into labour only two weeks later, at the peak of the monsoon season. I arrived at about lunch time, without troubling my dear mater too much, and was instantly named Madhav, with nominal ceremony.

Protima *mashi* congratulated my parents jubilantly at my arrival. With me as a conspicuous proof of the astrologer's authenticity, Protima *mashi* became an even more ardent believer in destiny. She went to all the right temples, and made all the right offerings to all the right deities. She regularly brought us prasad. She massaged my limbs and bathed me, while my mother tried to catch a wink or two after a hectic night trying to sing me to sleep.

In the afternoons, she would still entertain her little monkey brigade of the society, at her residence. She would prepare mouth-watering Bengali delicacies for them as they spread the *chotaai* on the floor in the living room and laid out the carom coins. She would seat herself beside them and play with them, and throw her usual tantrum when they cheated and won a game.

'Just wait, you rascals! When my daughter is born, she'll pay all of you back with interest for your naughtiness! Just you wait!'

'How do you know your child will be a daughter, *mashi*?' the boys would snicker. 'Don't you think a boy would do the job better?'

But *mashi* remained unruffled.

'No!' she spoke categorically. 'My child will be a daughter . . . you wait and see. She'll be stronger and smarter than any of you brats! She'll outclass you any day!'

Protima *mashi* traced the footprints of her ancestors right down to Raja Ram Mohan Roy and beyond, in some vague, convoluted manner, but she was very proud of the connection.

'We Bongs are very proud of our culture,' she said. 'And our literary heritage, of course. My ancestors were broadminded people and encouraged women's education. I can read and write well. My daughter will do better! She won't land up as a typist or PA like her father, or a housewife like her mother. No, sir! She will be a doctor, a professor ... or maybe an IAS officer?' she said hopefully, looking at her husband.

'Yeah ... a scholar with genes from intellectual cripples like you and I!' Her husband laughed. 'Sure as hell!'

'I'll name her Arunima,' *mashi* said happily. 'How do you like the name, Mr Roy?'

'I think Mouli is a better name,' answered her husband. 'So sweet. My grandmother was Mouli. And she was such a lovely woman. We'll name our daughter after her.'

'No, Arunima!' Protima *mashi* said stubbornly.

'Mouli!'

'Arunima!'

The argument continued ad infinitum.

She became well known for her tempestuous outbursts. She raged, she raved, she ranted. Almost nobody escaped her biting tongue, which she brandished like an Indian *shamshir*. Depending on her mood, the victim could be anybody from her cretinous cook crouching in the kitchen, to the crestfallen electrician who turned up late for a repair. The frenzied, sibilant sounds in varying decibels reached and tickled the neighbours' ears quite often. She was as munificent as she was temperamental. One day, she would scream at the cook and almost banish her from the house for good. The next day, she would donate a whole wardrobeful of old clothes to her for her children.

There was one thing that could put Protima *mashi* in good humour anytime. Yes, fish—the enchanting anodyne and antidote to any malady. It is erroneous to assume that all Bengalis find this aquatic palate seducer irresistible. I know more Bengalis who cannot stand the mention of fish than those who swear their lasting devotion to it. However, for *mashi*, it was that *sanjeevani booti* that could snatch her back from death; or transform her from stone to a live and kicking human being again, in case she ever ran into a gorgon. She made all these claims herself, by the way. God had endowed her with a febrile imagination, and he should know how generously she made use of it.

'... You should always check its bottom,' she would coach her husband about fish buying. 'If it's pink, it means that the fish is fresh. If it is blue or bluish green, then you know that the fish is a stale one.'

'What!' Mr Roy recoiled in horror. 'There's no way I'm going to spend my time studying the buttocks of a fish, Protima!'

'But you must!' she replied earnestly. 'How will you catch a lying fish seller otherwise?'

'Protima, please! I've done enough strange things for your sake, but I draw the line here ... ' Mr Roy would declare and walk away. 'Imagine ... does a fish even *have* buttocks?'

Doi maach, maacher jhol, Chingri maacher kofta, Bengali Fish Fry ... you name it, and she knew at least forty-five recipes to prepare it, by heart.

We were families from different parts of Delhi, UP, Punjab, and surrounding states in that society. There were even a handful of Malayalis and Tamilians. Strange though it may sound, we had never had any Bengali neighbours. The Roys were our first. And of course, it was simply a matter of time before Protima *mashi* miraculously combed out a few more erstwhile unobtrusive members of her clan from the surrounding flats. The number kept burgeoning with surprising speed. Like popcorns they popped out of thin air—the Ghoses, Mukherjees, Banerjees, Chatterjees, Guptas, and Senguptas.

There is a popular belief that where three Bengalis meet, there is a Durga Puja. Protima *mashi* was bent upon proving it. She assumed complete responsibility for the event and formed a tiny committee planning, organising, collecting funds, and recruiting new members such as my mother, and young volunteers from her worshipping monkey brigade.

Whereas so far our society used to reverberate with huge, clamorous loud speakers belching dissonant screeches all through the celebrations during October, that *navaratri*, they witnessed something new at their very own doorstep: a rainbow display of puja pandals and shaamiyanas, carpets, and fancy portals zestfully competing with each other; regal Durga *protima*s being installed in each, accompanied by Mahisasur, Kartik, Ganesha, Saraswati, and Lakshmi; palate pampering aromas wafting from nearby houses—*khichchudi*, *chaana*, *sondesh*, *shiuli*; *pujor-thaala* and smoking censers; heavily accented voices hesitantly rasping about cultural competitions for children over the microphone: a veritable *mela* of sound, smell, and colour intoxicating the five senses.

Arnab was born on Vijaya Dashmi… Dussera day for us.

'*Shubho Bijoya*,' said an obviously awed voice from the mighty throng, and before Protima *mashi* could cheerfully return the greeting, or stop to compliment herself on her stupendous achievement, the throes had begun.

His arrival was as unexpected as the scientists' discovery that the earth was round. So far, Protima *mashi* had indeed believed hers to be square. Arnab opened his infant eyes to the exhilarated shouts of '*Shubho Bijoya*!' and 'Jai Sri Ram!' while his parents digested the news of his arrival in cemetery-like silence.

My mother sent out the happy news to all Protima *mashi*'s relatives and friends. Mother painstakingly prepared *besan laddoo*s at home and distributed them to all the friends and neighbours. She took care of protocol while Protima *mashi* seemed to have slipped into a state of semi-consciousness, intensified further after the pokerfaced doctor pronounced that she could plan another pregnancy only at the risk of her own life. They brought the solemn-looking little bundle home, wrapped in a pink towel *mashi* had lovingly chosen for their daughter-to-arrive. He was given the *dak naam* Anu, for Bengalis seem to have a penchant for nicknames.

Arnab was a strange child—silent, dreamy, withdrawn. He didn't do any of the wild things boys of his age usually do—the things my friends and I did. While we would wildly throw ourselves upon the little hillocks of sand and bricks at a construction site near our society, roll over wrestling with our friends soaking our school uniform with filth, and pick out diminutive shells from the little silver dunes on our way back from school, Arnab would walk past us, daydreaming. He would dutifully put his books in place, wash his hands, change his uniform, eat his lunch, and then saunter alone to a dried up ditch behind the society where a brown stray had given birth to a litter of seven. He would park himself upon a large boulder and watch them, fascinated. At other times, he trudged up to the little bridge on a small arm of a river not too far off, and stood on it for hours, staring at the rippling water underneath.

It wasn't as though we didn't make an effort to be friends with him. But somehow, it never seemed to register. We were just indistinguishable, invisible shapes in the sand, washed away by the rippling river. Given the close bond between Protima *mashi* and my mother, it was usually taken for granted that Arnab and I must be best friends. I could never explain to such people how incorrect their assumptions were. Arnab and I could not have been more different, for I loved company, loved to be wild, and almost never listened to my parents. Goaded by my mother, my friends and I made attempts again and again to involve him in our games, but unsuccessfully.

And yet, those dark eyes often gazed at me steadily when we were alone, till I finally turned away from them. It did not happen too often, but often enough to make me feel uncomfortable. They unsettled me, those dark eyes. They were soft, almost liquid—the kind that pierce your soul with their simple honesty.

Once Anuj, Prashant, and I were intensely involved in a thrilling game towards nightfall. While the adults enjoyed a quiet dinner inside somebody's warm house shielded from the cold, the three of us were left behind outside near the easy chairs, minding the dying embers of the bonfire they had just enjoyed together. As we sat back on the cold floor, chatting, Prashant saw a couple of black ants moving in a single file on the wall he was leaning against. His eyes suddenly brightened.

'Let's burn the ants,' he said to us eagerly. 'It's fun, you know.'

'Really?' Anuj was as curious as I was.

'Yeah,' said our knowledgeable friend, talking down to the pair of imbeciles. 'It can't hurt them. They're not humans like us, are they? They just shrivel in the fire. It's funny to see them trying to run away.'

'Are you ... are you quite sure, Prashant?' I said, not wishing to face my mother's wrath later.

My other two more brawny friends laughed at me.

'Come on, tender heart!' They squealed. 'Don't tell us you're afraid.'

'Who's afraid?' I said, indignantly. 'Come on, I was only trying to test your courage. Let's go.'

Prashant was the first one to lift a wriggling little black organism from the ground and drop it into the fire. It shrivelled up immediately. All at once, his devilry propelled the other two to imitate him. And we did ... scared at first, but then slowly getting bolder, we became more adroit at the task, the adrenalin surging more freely as the evening quickly progressed. In a short while, the stimulating game had transformed into an insane contest, with each of us desperately trying to outdo the other two. As we continued our madness laughing like lunatics, not one of us noticed the tiny figure silently gliding across the wall, standing with a soda ash face, witnessing our crime, horrorstruck and robbed of speech.

'Hey, run!' Prashant yelped, suddenly catching a glimpse of the eyewitness.

'What? What happened?' we yelled back, confused.

'Nothing. There's that namby-pamby crybaby over there watching us,' said Prashant dryly. 'He'll tell on us!'

'Why, that's Arnab!' I said, feeling suddenly guilty and uncomfortable.

'Precisely. It's that soft sissy. Now run before he recognises you!'

An overriding feeling of panic caught hold of all three of us, and we ran, leaving Arnab to his cold, hysterical sobs. Though we ran for our lives that night, I was more than certain that Arnab had seen and recognised me. I couldn't stop worrying about those dark eyes filled with tears, watching us ... watching me. It was almost as though I had committed some kind of treachery. The discomfiting thought haunted me all through the chilly night, making it impossible for me to fall asleep. I contemplated upon my actions, part angry, part anxious, surprised at my own sadism, guilty at my own brutality. What if Arnab complained to my parents? I dared not think about my father's temper. What if he told Protima *mashi*, and she spoke to my mother about it? That thought too was equally disconcerting.

I need not have worried. Arnab never told on me. He never told on anybody.

When we were a little older, Protima *mashi* decided to throw a fancy dress party for the restless monkey brigade of the society. All the children below twelve years of age were cordially invited. She announced that the winner would receive a special reward. As usual, she went bananas deciding upon an attractive prize and bought one from the money-collection left over from last time's miscellany. She threw herself at the task with complete zest. And, as usual, a wave of buoyant anticipation swept through our society. Excited children and hyper-excited parents swarmed over the local market searching for fresh ideas, and fresh looks. The invitation sent my mother into a tizzy as well.

'Fancy dress? Where do I get a fancy dress for you now? Wonder what she's going to dress Arnab up as. That boy hardly has any life ... tch tch ... and to think he isn't six months younger to my son.'

Mother was muttering more to herself, but that was an interesting question. None of us had spared a thought for Arnab so far. I wondered what he would be dressed up as. There was a huge question mark on his presence. Having known him for so long, I doubted he would be anywhere around ... and even if he were, I couldn't imagine him as an active participant in any event. He was too much of a person of another world, too much of a stranger to our own. Sometimes, just sometimes, my heart bled for him. Somehow those dark, velvet eyes always struck me. But I dared not show it in front of another soul.

Mother dressed me up as a village farmer in an off white dhoti and a turban. With my swarthy skin and lean build, I believe I did complete justice to the character. There were several others—policemen, clowns, statues, puppets, actors, doctors, gardeners, and dancers. There was one child no one could immediately recognise. Dressed in a long, blue evening gown wrapped sensuously around each curvature of his body, wearing a plum frost lipstick, and thick mascara over curling eyelashes, balancing himself precariously upon golden high heels, stood—Arnab. I gasped. The others in the crowd did too. Protima *mashi* seemed to have spent more than a few hours working assiduously upon his makeover. He looked like an elegant neuter, standing shyly in a corner, staring into a void.

Instantly, fear gripped me. 'Arnab, no!' I wanted to scream. 'Go back inside, you idiot! Don't you know those wolves out there will devour you?'

I moved, quickly, urgently towards him—and halted all of a sudden. Was I just being paranoid about nothing? Did I have any right to interfere, really? What if I didn't? After all, it *was* a fancy dress competition, wasn't it?

Should I; shouldn't I? I wasted five minutes wrestling with myself. Just as I decided I should call out to him, I realised he had moved out of his hiding place. He was walking straight into the ground, in the middle of all those waiting people.

The hooting was instantaneous.

'Arnab is a girl! Arnab is a girl!' a little girl ran singing to her mother.

'Mum, come and see! Everybody, come and see! Arnab is a girl!'

'Hey you, crybaby! Started bawling already, have you?'

Mortified beyond any words could ever express, Arnab stood exposed to their relentless jeers and malicious remarks, their vitriolic tongues scissoring his heart into a million strips. Protima *mashi* and I looked on dismally, making an abortive attempt to silence the crowd.

'Madho!' She called to me for help in misery. 'Stop those stupid boys!'

But the poisoned arrows had already left the bow and gashed his soul.

'Come on, you rascals!' *mashi* chided them. 'Don't you have any manners? Where's your sense of humour? Anu has been so sporting and this is how you receive him!'

The voices died down instantly, though low murmurs and snickering behind his back still continued. To say that Arnab had no part in the catastrophic event, except that he bowed before his enthusiastic parent's desire, would be futile. And yet, that is precisely what he did. As a dutiful son, he always bowed before his parents' wishes unquestioningly.

Hain, ma.

Hain, baba.

Objection and retaliation were words outside his vocabulary. And characteristically, once again, when his mater expressed her wish, he said '*Hain, ma.*'

'Good boy,' she said, pleased.

'Will *baba* be pleased, *ma*?'

'Yes, yes, he will; don't you worry. He'll be very pleased.'

That was it.

The sun, and rain, and cold fused into each other year after year, without any of us taking much notice. I was still a skeletal, average-height figure in my teens. Arnab had grown a few notches taller than I now. His muscular chest, long locks, and serene eyes made him look like the leading actor of some mythological film. He still wandered on lonesome terrains all by himself. He still stood on the little bridge over the little rivulet, staring at the rippling water below. He went to school, all right. He pored over his books religiously, and scraped through his exams each time, but his mind was elsewhere. Once when he failed his math exam just before the boards, his father got rather perturbed.

'Anu, this cannot go on,' he said to his son, who stood in front of him, head bowed. 'Do you understand me? You will make us the laughing stock of this society if you fail your boards.'

'*Hain, baba*.'

'I've heard there's a teacher ... a Professor Chatterjee, who lives in the colony two blocks away. He's supposed to be a very good math tutor. I think we'll engage you as his pupil.'

'*Hain, baba*.'

Professor Chatterjee's house was one of the old world *haveli*s, with uniform rooms on all four sides and an open quadrangle in the centre. Arnab was asked to wait outside, while Mr Roy followed the servant humbly inside. Arnab slipped to the ground, and lounged himself with his back against the wall, staring idly at the flapping items on the clothesline in the wind. A dulcet sound of ringing *ghungroo*s snapped him awake from his daydream.

'*Tat tat ta* ...' a male voice counted the beats.

He turned to see the Kathak teacher demonstrating the dance steps to a nice-looking, young, obviously uninterested figure standing before him in the quadrangle.

'... *draigye*,' the teacher continued, demonstrating a movement of a finger gracefully around the eyes, '*thun thun* ...' Two lotuses in front.

Arnab sat up watching the forceful-graceful body language, the elastic movement of the torso and neck swaying left to right, and right to left to the rhythm; and the graceful hands showing different gestures... hypnotised.

'*Didi taike to tamang, taike thun thun...*' sang the teacher gaining rhythm, '*digda digdig thai...*'

There he completed a graceful rotation on his toes, with his hands forming a lotus over his head.

'*Maadho ek*!' The teacher sat down with the tabla again, while his young pupil followed his steps unhappily, dragging her feet—resisting, bored.

'I can't do it, guru ji,' the young girl whimpered complainingly. 'I can't do the rotations. I get a headache.'

'Nonsense!' said the teacher. 'Try it again... seriously this time. You'll get it right with practice.'

Awestruck, Arnab walked into the quadrangle. Silently, he took his position next to the young learner. He touched the earth before him in reverence, and stood with both his elbows upright, hands perfectly in position.

The teacher began once again. And along with the young learner, Arnab's beautiful body moved—stimulated, enthused, vigorous—in perfect motion, rhyme and rhythm—naturally responding to the stirring beat of the musical instrument. His light feet caught the beat easily, toes and heels working in concert; his hands instinctively glided up, down, east, and west, his fingers elegantly imitating the gestures to perfection; and his neck moved like a sinuous spring moving a clay puppet's head. To an ordinary eye, he was an enchanted *devadasi* absorbed in divine worship. There they sat together, Arnab, the serpent; the tabla, the snake charmer.

'Digda digdig thai ... digda digdig thai ... digda digdig thai ...'

'Digda digdig thai ... digda digdig thai ... digda digdig thai ...'

'Digda digdig thai ... digda digdig thai ... digda digdig ... ta thai thai tat ...'

'Beautiful! Simply beautiful!' Arnab heard an unfamiliar voice articulate in sincere appreciation, and he turned around to see Professor Chatterjee's well-built body standing next to his muted father (whose vocal chords seemed to have suffered a brief paralysis).

'Well done, my boy,' Professor Chatterjee continued. 'Well done! I'm so pleased. You're so much better than my daughter!' He winked at his piqued daughter. The young pupil made a face at the modest gathering and ran away. 'I think you need Kathak lessons more than you need training in numbers. Right, guru ji?'

The Kathak teacher bowed, smiling.

'Isn't he a natural, guru ji?'

'Absolutely, dada,' guru ji replied softly.

'You see, Mr Roy,' he said, talking to Arnab's father, 'that's what he's made for. Didn't you see his grace, his body language? He seemed to be so absorbed. Sublime.'

They walked home in silence, father and son. Where there should have been glowing pride in the father's heart, Mr Roy's heart had only gathered offence. How dare Professor suggest such insanity! He had no right to humiliate him thus! He huffed and he puffed, and he fumed for a few days. He resolutely refused to allow his son any dance lessons, classical or otherwise.

'Hain, that's all that's left!' He said to Protima *mashi* angrily. 'He's already brought so much ridicule upon us. Now you want him to bring more?'

'Well, all right. But how will you explain it to him?'

'There's nothing to explain,' replied Mr Roy categorically. Facing his son, he said, 'No Kathak lessons for you, Anu…not now, not ever! Do you get me, my boy?'

'*Hain, baba.*'

Anything to please baba. If it required the passion of his life he had just discovered, to be stubbed under the toe like a cigarette, he would do that too.

The math tuition, however, began in earnest as the board exams neared. Professor Chatterjee was patient, interesting, and articulate. He had a whole squad of students of all ages brimming over his little classroom. He would spend a little time with each, answering their queries, and then leave them alone to continue while he concentrated on someone else. Arnab made use of these little breaks watching the Kathak teacher teach new pieces to Nupur (for that was the name of Professor Chatterjee's young daughter).

Though all of us passed our exams with more or less a decent result, Arnab's math tuitions did not stop. He was always lagging behind in the subject and, in spite of Professor Chatterjee's most excellent efforts, seemed to be making no substantial progress. I thought I should try to help, but his very aura intimidated me. I was far superior to him as a student. But somehow, his disconnectedness with the world, and all those in it, awed me. I could never approach him and say, 'Come on, good fellow, let me give you a hand with some sums.'

The idea was absurd. But he seemed to understand it. Many a time I saw those molten eyes look warmly at me, smiling.

Arnab's interest in Kathak did not wane. Dancing was a massage for his soul. He forgot all tribulations of the world when the tabla sounded, and the pleasant tinkling of *ghungroo* bells filled his ears. He became the leading dancer at the aarti during the Durga Puja celebrations. He would dance as though possessed, his feet catching beat upon beat, his hand waving the smoking censer around expertly. He moved with such exceptional grace that people stopped to watch, awestruck.

As the new term began, the teachers began to lighten up a little. There was more spare time to indulge in sports and extra-curricular activities. The class teacher walked in one day, and cheerfully announced that all the students had to opt for a hobby class. The classes would be held once every week. She began to write the options on the blackboard, while all the classmates murmured amongst themselves discussing what they would like to register for. Only Arnab sat on a back bench, oblivious to the clamour in the classroom, gazing vacantly outside at a wilted flower.

At the end of the period, the teacher had everybody's preferences sorted.

'Arnab!' she called his name.

He turned towards her, unspeaking.

'Arnab, I've called your name at least ten times during the class, and you haven't answered.'

'Sorry, ma'am,' he mumbled standing up, with his head bowed.

'All the children have given me their preferences already. You still haven't ... and now, most of the slots are already filled up anyway.' She seemed to be considering something. 'All ... except the needlework class.'

The class sniggered.

'It's a stitching and embroidery class, I know, and no boys ever opt for it, but the principal will not like it if nobody from our class enrolls for it and, in any case, I can't find place for you anywhere else. I'm putting your name up for this, all right?'

More sniggering.

'Yes, ma'am,' replied Arnab with a bow.

Arnab took to needlework like nostrils to oxygen. He continued his stitching and embroidery lessons right through school and university, in spite of his father. Concealed from his father's eye, he sat for hours delighting in needlework with his mother.

'Will *baba* be pleased, ma?'

'Yes, yes, he loved the cushion you did. He just loved it!' Protima *mashi* gloated in front of her son. 'Just don't mention to him that *you* did it, all right?'

Several laced handkerchiefs and table covers ascribed to his mother eventually turned out to be Arnab's own handiwork. They were flawless pieces of a craftsman's proficient hands. He could infuse life into any fabric with the shades of his natural gift. He could fill the softest Pashmina shawls with the most intricate patterns and emphasise the effect with pulsating colours, working his hands like a true maestro. He could embroider breathtaking designs on the most sinuous silk—a feat even few experts managed to achieve.

Mr Roy, when he discovered the truth, did not know where to look. Suddenly, the giant pink and white embroidered roses on his favourite mustard table cloth, that he used to love so much once upon a time, seemed to wilt in front of his eyes. He thundered at his son. 'Will become a seamstress, yeah? Will become a seamstress! Won't study and get a degree, or be responsible enough to get a job!'

He shouted, cracking a cane on Arnab's knee. 'How will you make a living when we are gone? I won't be around to feed you forever, *boojhte parish*? *Boka gaadha*!'

Another whack!

Arnab winced.

'Oh, that I should have ever prayed for a daughter!' Mr Roy lamented. Protima *mashi* flinched.

'Study for god's sake, you rotter!'

'*Hain*, *baba*. I thought it might please you, *baba*...'

'Please me!' Mr Roy was incredulous. 'Please me, eh? You wretched idiot!'

Silent tears stung Arnab's eyes, as he sat in remote corners, but Arnab never retaliated in front of his parents.

Arnab soon discovered another delight. He didn't need to learn recipes. They poured from him—original, appetising, perfect. He shared the zeal for catering with his mother in the kitchen, in the absence of his father. He could prepare absolutely anything from meat to rice, to *luchi*s, to Mughlai, to continental food. He could craft lasagna as easily as he could prepare *maacher jhol or sondesh*. And he developed a fetish for fish just like his mother.

'This is bound to please *baba*, isn't it, *ma*? *Baba* loves his *doi maach*.'

'*Hain, shona*,' said *mashi* smiling. '*Akdum*.'

And so it did. The *doi maach* that day slid down his pater's throat with leisurely ease, making him smack his lips in appreciation. Good food and a full tummy does wonders to one's temper. Arnab and his mother decided to keep their secret a secret. Why invite the bull to charge unnecessarily when one could help it?

One Monday morning, Mr Roy announced that Professor Chatterjee was organising a lunch for the whole society. He required help. Mr Roy asked Arnab to visit Neela, a neighbourhood cook, and convey the message to her.

'*Hain, baba*,' Arnab returned, and obliged. But not finding Neela at home, he decided to head for Professor Chatterjee's house himself.

Nobody questioned his presence there, of course. Standing amongst the huge containers, and pots and pans, with the other cooks, he absentmindedly began to assist them in their work until, after a few minutes, the roles were reversed.

'*Bah*! What perfect round *luchi*s, dada!' said the head cook in wonder. 'Even I, with years of experience behind me, cannot turn out such mouthwatering *luchi*s! Where did you learn the art?'

Arnab smiled, and the chef left, shaking his head.

He was still working at the hot, round *luchi*s dexterously when he heard sweet, wind chime laughter at his side. There stood Nupur, Professor Chatterjee's youthful daughter, batting her doe eyes coquettishly at him.

'*Ooh ma, ki korcho tumi*, Arnab?' she asked with a seductive smile, swaying her rope-like plait playfully. *What are you doing, Arnab*?

Arnab continued to work, not paying any attention to the distraction.

'*Oodi baba, ki* concentration!' she mocked, laughing.

'*Tumi kono kaaj kaino korcho na*?' said Arnab in return, pretending to be indignant. *Why aren't you doing any work*?

Nupur laughed her sweet wind chime laugh again. '*Bah*!' she said, '*Ki moja*!' *Oh, what fun*!

Arnab returned to his work, not taking any further notice of the young woman. Not happy at being ignored so casually, calculating young Nupur intentionally dropped a clay pot half filled with lukewarm oil standing behind Arnab, on her foot. She screamed as though a vicious shark had caught her limb in its mouth. Almost instantly, Arnab leapt to his feet and, deserting that lot of *luchi*s to their fate, he was at her side, taking her apparently injured foot in his hands, and pouring cold water over it. It was at this moment that Professor Chatterjee made a sudden, unexpected appearance at the venue of the turmoil.

Nobody knew exactly why Arnab's visits to Professor Chatterjee's household abruptly ceased. There were many whispers, many conjectures though.

'Don't you know? Arnab … yeah *that* Arnab … caught with Professor's daughter … .'

'Hush! How can it be? That androgynous poltroon?'

'Yeah.'

'Hee hee, come on! Impossible! Don't you know he's—?'

Giggle, giggle, snicker, snicker.

Arnab remained unflustered. He continued his liaison with his tabla and *ghungroo*s, needle and thread, wok and spatula, as he always had—in a frenzied, trancelike state. Mr Roy was fury incarnate.

'See? See what this boy has come to!' He raged at home. 'A nautch girl, a seamstress, and a good-for-nothing sod! Even after his graduation he's sitting idle at home, dreaming all day long! Irresponsible rascal! *Kono kormer na*! None of this any more, all right? I'm taking you to Bijoy babu this instant. Maybe he'll be able to find you a clerk's job somewhere. That's all you are fit for, foolish fellow! And to think we had such dreams!'

Silence reigned. Arnab stood before his thundering father, head bowed as usual.

'*Cholo*,' said Mr Roy, standing up from his chair, brushing his kurta. 'You're coming with me right now!'

Arnab's dark eyes were fearful.

'*Hain, baba*.'

They came to our house thus that day. My father, Dr Vijay Bajpayee, was an esteemed physician of the society. He had spent several fruitful years serving humanity at the local government hospital. Some of his erstwhile patients landed up at our residence once in a while even now, asking for him. However, he had made use of the voluntary retirement scheme, and was now running his modest practice within the precincts of our society. It was much less strenuous, and it provided the family just enough to keep us going. But then, my father had never been the hyper-ambitious kind.

Mr Roy arrived that day, quite literally, with folded hands and a hopeless expression in his eyes. My father had no option but to promise him sincerely that he would find a suitable job for Arnab. Mother and I exchanged worried glances a few times during the entire conversation. My heart was madly sinking again. By this time I knew that Arnab indeed was a misfit in our real, corporeal world. His flight was the flight of a turtle dove in the limitless mauve expanse. And I was afraid that his wonderful feathers were about to be ruthlessly severed... and severed by his own kith and kin, the people he called his family and friends.

Father found him employment at Mr Murti's law firm, as an assistant to Mr Murti's own personal assistant. All day long, he had to sit in a dingy, almost windowless square cubicle—a dozen feet long and a dozen feet wide, crammed with rusty, old exposed shelves, piled with moth-eaten heavy files audaciously baring their tattered intestines to the stranger's eyes. It was Arnab's job to take a soiled duster and wipe them clean, and rearrange them neatly on the shelves in the order of the English alphabet. An impossible task really, since most of the files either lacked a cover altogether, or the ink spelling out the relevant information was too washed out to be intelligible. It was robotic, mindless work, morning to evening, day after day, sitting caged in that airless space, arranging redundant files. It was a homicidal decree for a vulnerable soul like Arnab's. And I believe it did destroy him somehow, somewhere.

I don't really know how long Arnab served his sentence imprisoned within those soul-demolishing walls for, by this time, I had left the city to proceed to Banaras for higher education. I had made it to Banaras Hindu University, and was happy with my feat. But when I returned home next, I found Protima *mashi* in a state of great enthusiasm. She was back to her old self, her baby face grinning as though she'd found a treasure under her bed that morning, her bright eyes sparkling. I could tell there was something in the air from the conspiratorial whispering and shush-shushing whenever she and my mother were alone. Neither bothered to enlighten me, however, nor did I bother to enquire.

It was not too many days later that Mr Roy and his wife decided upon a chat with Arnab. He had quit Mr Murti's office and, at least for a little while, had been absorbed as a teacher in a local high school. What he taught, nobody knew. Protima *mashi* claimed it was Hindi, though I had a strong suspicion it might have been needlecraft or Kathak. And if so, my heart was glad for him. He never mentioned it. Arnab was still the same solitude-loving soul, and I left him to it. But apparently, his reprieve didn't last too long. According to the rumours, the minute his father discovered his son's true occupation, Arnab was roughly hauled out of the school, and apprenticed as a clerk in another airless pigeonhole in another soul-demolishing government office.

'Anu…' his senior parent began, as Protima *mashi* plonked herself on the bed nearby, dangling her feet eagerly. 'You are old enough now…'

Arnab stared at them, uncomprehending.

'We… your *ma* and *baba*, think that it's time for you to settle down in life… get married, raise a family…'

Comprehension now dawned upon him.

'I don't want to get married, *baba*,' said Arnab quietly. For the very first time ever in the history of his own life, Arnab uttered that single syllable 'no', and his parents gasped.

'What do you mean? You won't get married?' Protima *mashi* was promptly at his side, nudging him, chiding him. 'I know just the girl for you. Chaitali, Dr Sugata Sen's daughter in Kolkata. Beautiful girl ... and such qualities too.'

'*Ma, hobe na*,' returned the visibly disturbed son, lamely.

'*Hobe*, *hobe*!' said Protima *mashi*, clapping her hands teasingly. 'She'll make such a good wife! You'll look so good together, both of you! *Bah*, *ki moja*!'

'No, *ma* ... you ... you don't understand!'

'I'll fix it up, don't you worry. Come on, child, we are your parents. Don't we know what's good for you? You need a wife ... and I'll get you an ideal girl, all right?'

The last rays of the afternoon sun withdrew quietly from the little balcony outside, leaving the house in semi-darkness. The nip in the air became more palpable as the warmth disappeared from the room with the last rays of daylight, and Arnab shuddered in the cold.

'*Hain*, *ma*,' Arnab replied with a resigned bow.

None of us had ever witnessed a Bengali wedding before either. No one at all. The news had an immediate effect upon our society. Preparations began in each house on a colossal scale. Though weddings are largely family affairs, Protima *mashi* dragged my mother everywhere along with her. She refused to take no for an answer. To her, my mother was more 'family' than her own family.

And so it happened that my mother also accompanied her to meet the prospective bride's family in Kolkata.

'But Proti... if Anu isn't willing, do you think this is wise?' she asked, hesitating, not sure whether it was a right question. But *mashi* waved her worries away airily.

'Don't worry, didi. I know my Anu. He's just shy, that's all. He'll be all right.'

Chaitali *boudi* (bhabhi as she was called in our part of the world) was a stark contrast to her baby mother-in-law. She was tall for one thing, almost as tall as Arnab, and almost as broad. But her limbs were gracefully formed, and her beautiful face exuded warmth and prudence.

Mother was an active participant in the *ashirwad* ceremony, and in the *alpana*; in the selection of the bride's saris with all their appurtenances; and in buying and organising the fish, sweets, curd, *paan*, and the works, to be gifted to the bride and her huge family. My parents were especially invited for the pre-wedding ceremonies—the *adhibas tattva*, the *kubi patta*, and numerous other rituals which they were neither familiar with nor really understood very well, since nobody had the time to translate it all for them. But they enjoyed all of it anyhow. To my inexperienced eyes, it was a kaleidoscopic fusion of colours, food, and rituals which came and went like a hurricane. And all through the hurricane, Arnab sat quietly—distant, detached, dreaming—an outsider at his own wedding.

Feeling almost sorry for him, I went up to him once. He was sitting all by himself in a lonely corner of the garden, lost in thought.

'Anu,' I was afraid to rouse him from his dream.

He looked up, surprised—and surprised me. There were angry tears in those eyes. Seeing me, he became more restless. His fingers twitched; his body trembled.

'Anu, what's wrong?' I was genuinely concerned.

'Madho!' The eyes showed sheer agony. 'Even you betrayed me, Madho.'

The words stung me.

'Me?'

'Yes, *you*. I thought—I thought you understood!' he cried, taking my hands in his. He pressed them so hard that they hurt.

I stared at the anguish in those dark eyes, open-mouthed. I remembered the same eyes I had seen gazing at me so many years ago ... those serene, penetrating eyes.

Shocked, I pulled my hands away, mumbling something incoherent. I wasn't watching where I was going, as I turned away to flee. God! Dear god! How could I have been so wretchedly blind all these years? What a disaster! I could feel Arnab's body still trembling behind me as I moved away, feeling worse than I ever had in my entire life. Anu! Anu! Anu ... What ... *How*? A second later I heard an agonised cry behind me, but did not dare to look back. I felt dazed; my eyes were hazy. As I ran my fingers across my face absently, I realised my eyelashes were wet too.

It wasn't even seven days since the wedding when Arnab disappeared. He vanished suddenly, without saying a word to a soul, even to his newly wedded wife. The search went on for days.

'Arnab ... of course! I saw him with a passing dance troupe that night, travelling past our society,' said Vivek, a local vendor. 'How could I not recognise those long locks and that muscular body dancing so gracefully? Of course it was him!'

'Oh no! I saw him at the railway station. Those tranquil eyes... Of course that had to be him!'

'Arnab, Arnab, Arnab... wasn't that the name that mad beggar at Ghanta Ghar was chanting the other day? I'm sure he had something to do with his disappearance.'

They found a body in the river the third day after the search began—a tall structure with a muscular chest, long locks, and serene eyes. The corpse had taken its time to come up and reveal itself to a lone searcher who had strayed farther than he intended.

Mr Roy was quietly sent for to identify the body. My father and I escorted him to the mortuary disbelievingly. Mr Roy stared at the bloated body, and facial features distorted beyond recognition. His hands trembled as he stood there gazing at the shapely features of the body—the hands, the legs, the feet. A *craftsman's* hands. A *dancer's* feet. I had a sudden, inexplicable urge to scream my lungs out, but couldn't cough up a word. I had an invisible hangman's noose tight round my neck.

Some moisture glistened at the edges of Mr Roy's greying brows. He did not speak, though it seemed as if his knees too had begun to wobble a little. In a few minutes that blurred by, he stepped back and steadied himself, still silent. He wasn't trembling now. He lingered on at the site, the sand and silt reflecting the ash-grey emotions in his eyes. He studied the serene corpse till he could look at it no more. The uncomplaining onlookers stood waiting for him to speak. But there was silence. Only silence. One of the boatmen busied himself shrouding the body with a thick, white cloth.

Mr Roy shook his head slowly after deliberating for a long, long time.

'No,' he whispered at last. 'Not my son.'

Disbelief crossed my face. My father flopped by my side. And yet, we couldn't blame him. He was the father after all. He had lived his whole life with his son, watching him laugh, cry, fall sick, and grow up. He should know. Even if none of us did, he would.

It was also a relief to us. In some corner of our heart, hope still remained. And yet, there was a niggling feeling—that invisible, intangible *thing* that will not let you rest in peace even when everything seems well on the surface.

Who knows if the pale images of the distorted face lying tranquilly upon the grey soil near the riverbed ever haunted Mr Roy's dreams? They haunted mine.

Nobody knew that Arnab had not entered his wife's bedroom that wedding night. Nobody knew that Arnab had not entered his wife's bedroom any night. The wedding was a charade, in spite of his wife's virtuous and sincere efforts to begin a normal conjugal life. She never got to see her husband, never got to speak to him, never got to know him.

I believe *mashi*'s hysteria began a few days later. She held Chaitali *boudi* responsible for her son's disappearance. She was in denial.

'You!' she spat at her daughter-in-law. 'You drove him away, didn't you? All with your wiles and what not! You drove him away!'

'*Na, ma*, I didn't,' *boudi* replied quietly.

'Curse upon you, woman! You swallowed my only son!' *Mashi* cried exactly like someone from a sickening TV serial, and sent the tea tray flying across the room to land upon *boudi*'s feet.

Chaitali *boudi* left her in-laws' house silently the next day, and did not return—not when her father-in-law personally went to Kolkata to fetch her, begging forgiveness; not when I, accompanied by a few concerned friends, made an effort to bring her back; not when my mother accompanied Protima *mashi* to Kolkata to persuade her to return. She never did.

There was no stone Protima *mashi* and Roy *mesho* did not turn to locate their missing offspring. They went to the best astrologers in various parts of the country, and were informed that Arnab was a lonely destitute in some corner of Kochi; a beautiful craftsman embroidering saris in the heart of Jammu; a madman eating dust near the Golden Temple in Amritsar; a soulful dancer with a cluster of hermaphrodites at a red light area in Mumbai.

It had been a few years since that episode now. I hadn't had the heart to visit home during all this period. Though I had never really known Arnab, I still felt a pang in my heart whenever I thought of him. The thought was accompanied by a dull ache, and a strange feeling I could never quite define. Was it guilt? No, it was something more…even more than that. I had never been able to shake off that feeling ever since that day, epochs ago, when Arnab caught us burning ants in the fire.

She was half-lying, half-sitting on the patient's miniature expanse of a metal bed, cloaked in crumpled, white sheets of varying thickness. A combined smell of disinfectant, methylated spirit, and bitter medicine floated into my nostrils. On the other side, Mr Roy sat pensively on a stool, staring blankly at the wall opposite.

Her face broke into a smile when she saw me—the sunny pink smile of a summer cloud I remembered so well. She was still that petite pygmy woman, with her thick, unmanageable hair hugging her Edelweiss face. My heart leapt at her sight.

'*Mashi*!' I ran and hugged her. She laughed—a deep, resounding, contagious laugh of a happy waterfall gleefully sliding down its favourite slope.

'I knew you would come!' she said, her shapely Bengali eyes wrinkling into a chimp-like smile once again. Her delicately contoured eyelids reflected those of Goddess Durga, the most popular of Bengal's deities.

'Of course, I would have come!' I said, feeling embarrassed and indignant at the same time.

'See?' she said, turning towards her husband, 'See? Didn't I say he would come and bring me news of my son? You have heard from Anu, haven't you?' she asked, turning back to face me. 'He's written to you, surely? He's told you where he is, hasn't he?'

My heart suffered a blast at those innocent, hopeful words, and splintered into a million fragments. She continued to gaze at me, excited and expectant. Her eyes were brilliant lamps then … for those few moments, and I wished I could do something … anything … to keep them burning bright.

'No, *mashi*,' I said at last, taking her miniature hands in my own, 'I haven't heard from Arnab.'

Those lamps died out then. I saw the little hope flicker, and go out in one stroke—sharp and agonising. Her optimism fell like powder ash, spelling defeat, and the brawny throbbing mass in my chest suffered an excruciating cramp once more.

'Oh . . . ' she whispered. The soft miniature hands fell limp and lifeless in mine. The head drooped. Edelweiss withered again.

For a few minutes, she stayed silent. Then she raised her head once more.

'You are pulling my leg, aren't you?' she alleged, scanning my face for guilt.

'No, *mashi*, I am not,' I told her gently. She pulled her delicate hands away in disgust. Her eyes ladled out scorn and disdain in generous quantities. She busied herself with inaudible, incoherent murmurs addressed exclusively to herself. She was suddenly oblivious of the encompassing world.

I turned to Mr Roy. His face had a vacuous smile pasted on it. He folded his hands together, as if in apology . . . or perhaps greeting. Didn't he recognise me? I certainly hadn't altered so much. I was a grown up young man now with a job and a family, but that was about all. I couldn't comprehend it. But I guessed he was apologising on behalf of his wife, embarrassed at her behaviour. I writhed in embarrassment myself. This wasn't the couple I had known since birth—my *mashi* and *mesho*, my own extended family.

'It's all right, *mesho* . . . really. I . . . It's no problem at all,' I mumbled inanely.

He smiled, and turned away from me again.

'I shouldn't have let him go,' Protima *mashi* addressed me again. 'Did he love his mother, Madho?'

Those almonds were welling up with tears, and I was helpless to stop them. She whispered as though telling me a secret. 'He ran away. Do you know why? Because he hated us! He hated *me*!'

With each sentence, her voice grew louder, fiercer. She was slowly yielding to hysteria. Her husband sat glued to the stool, each muscle painfully carved in plasticine. He continued to stare at her quietly.

She turned to me again. 'So?' she said, waiting for an answer.

'*Mashi*?'

'I'm waiting. What did he say in his letter?'

'*Mashi*... I haven't received any letter.'

'I know you are lying. He's gone back to his wife, hasn't he? Ditched his mother to go back to his wife?'

'No, *mashi*,' I said softly but firmly. 'He hasn't gone back to his wife.'

'How do you know?' She was suddenly attacking. 'How do you know? He has written to you! You've been lying to me... all of you!'

She was agitated, and I knew any moment the matron or nurse might walk in and order me out.

'Ma has sent you something,' I said with a smile, deliberately diverting her mind. 'Some *luchi*s, *aaloo*, *paayesh*. Won't you have a look?'

She hesitated, and then laughed.

'Where is it? Let me have a look then.'

Her hands worked deftly, and she had the tiffin carrier open in less than a second. She foraged for hidden treasures and squealed when she found two *rosogulla*s tidily packed in a tiny bag, smuggled in with the *sabzi*. It broke my heart to see her gorge upon the meal my mother had so lovingly packed for her, with trembling hands.

'How's your child?' she asked me when she was through.

I fumbled with my old leather wallet in my trouser-pocket for a minute and pulled it out. I opened it to display the passport size photograph of my young daughter in front of her.

'Little Protima,' I said, smiling. 'We decided to name her after you, *mashi*.'

'Oh, my blessings upon the little soul!' Protima *mashi* exclaimed, touched. 'Give her my love.'

I stayed at the hospital for an hour, watching Protima *mashi* slide in and out of her make-believe world. I watched her silent husband spend that hour sitting by her bedside, fixed to his stool, patting the hysterical figure gently, arranging and rearranging her crumpled bed sheets. I didn't have the courage to stay on further. With moist eyes I took leave, promising Protima *mashi* (again and again as she made me) that I would visit her another time as soon as I received a letter from Arnab. I bowed a tearful goodbye to Mr Roy, still planted upon the stool, staring sadly back at me.

Stepping out of the room I ran into the doctor and, upon a whim, decided to snatch a few minutes of his time to clarify some of the doubts crawling in my mind.

'Yes,' said the doctor sighing. 'Psychosis. She's slowly losing her mind. The patient's deteriorating, I'm afraid.'

'What about her husband, doctor? Why does he look so strange?'

'The beginning of Alzheimer's,' said the doctor. 'A very tragic affair.'

Some memories rose from the mist the past had left behind in its wake; the night so many years ago: the brilliant dazzle and noise of wedding celebrations floating down the landing from the upstairs house in a happy diminuendo; the contrasting dim shadows throwing up ominous images on the pale walls of my own bedroom on the floor below; muffled mammal cries, luscious groans, sweaty-silky thighs locking and unlocking, the perfume of a fresh bridegroom's hair in my nostrils....

I stepped out into the evening mist, pulling the hood of my jacket over my head. My mind was a muddle. My numb feet walked on unconsciously, receiving jumbled signals from sluggish grey cells. The doctor's last phrase rang emptily in my brain coagulating into a lasting clot of empty words—a very tragic affair...a very tragic affair....

Turtle Dove

She lay on the four-poster bed naked as a newborn babe, her velvet pansy skin daubing the air with a dizzying aroma, inviting... egging him on. His artist eyes admiringly trailed the contours of her corporeal map, perfection incarnate, even with those occasional lumps of loose flab, even with that faint but permanent dark patch left behind by a jug of boiling water inadvertently upset ages ago. Her nose was a perfect stroke of an artist's fluid brush. Her soft lips were sweet molten ruby, eager... vulnerable. Enticing as crimson berries in the wilderness of the Himalayan range, they pulled him, against all reason, to their hypnotic lure. Her dazzle of a smile had enough warmth to make the sun blush. And he was too much of a mortal to resist.

It was the ebb and flow of love in her liqueur chocolate eyes that he found so mesmeric. A scoop of tenderness and warmth appeared in her soft glance, and then he saw it slowly melt... and then disappear completely. Her expression spelt half anguish, half challenge. She turned towards him, holding his unwavering gaze, unblinking, unthinking. She offered him her breasts ... ripe, succulent golden apples from Kashmir. His quavering hands cupped them gently, afraid to prick the dream bubble of the moment, and then ... slowly, hesitantly at first, then gaining momentum, his famished body succumbed to her.

His ravenous member groped the deep, yawning cavern of her being, hard, unyielding; lapping up the gooey nectar that gushed forth to clasp him, having waited for an agonising eternity, lavishing her love and aching desire frenziedly upon him—upon the fragment of his lacerated soul making a valiant effort to scramble back upon the sinking vessel of his life. Their bodies sashayed rhythmically, step by synchronised step—tongue to hungering tongue, bosom to tender bosom, spirit to raw spirit ... caressing, searching ... now warm, now wild; now vulnerable, now aggressive. Slowly and steadily, they vanished into the sound and fury of sense and sensuality.

'*Why*?' He whined at last, searching her eyes. 'Why?'

'Because I must,' she replied and turned over, only to be ruthlessly pulled back.

'Don't!' she begged, a pang stabbing her heart.

He released her. She turned away again, the babble of those crusty, gruff voices cramming her mind all over again. White noise.

'Mad, mad, raving mad, I say!' jeered one.

'Weirdo family!' hooted another. 'Mother was a whore!'

'Ran on the street naked once, did you hear that?' Raucous, derisive laughter.

She wrapped her hands around her ears, and brought her shuddering knees close together, closing her eyes, trying to block the killing recollection. She made a great effort to fight back a cloudburst of tears. But they poured. Her paramour pulled her to himself again, and held her tight. Being wrapped in his tight embrace felt like climbing under a snug duvet on a wintry night. All of a sudden, she could sense those convulsions returning, and she sobbed uncontrollably.

'It's all right, darling, it's all right,' he whispered kindly, his burly chest cradling her head. She hung on to him, and helplessly released the emotions she had been trying to keep under lock and key for so long.

'She was good, you know,' she uttered between sobs.

'I know,' he replied softly, sighing.

*****

Scene one. She is six years old. It's a Sunday morning. Her mother is sitting at her antique escritoire in the study room, writing. Sheets upon sheets of her manuscript are scattered all around her—random thoughts granted a free rein. Words swarm to her like children to a birthday cake. She writes with a neat hand, her letters forming oblique sans serif slashes in an orderly series. She is a great raconteur. She is usually happy when she has produced a good chapter. She is happy today one can make out since she is smiling pleasantly. She makes herself and her family cups of cappuccino periodically. She plays with her daughter often. Mummy is always writing. Her study room with her escritoire is her little hidey-hole in the mad world she lives in.

Her daddy stands distractedly on the terrace, facing the study room. His unrestrained imagination is exploring the miracles of the universe. A hundred wild horses gallop in his mind this way and that, seeking foreign landscapes and fresh adventures. He has put up his easel and placed a blank canvas upon it. He is holding a big, fat brush by his teeth, as he blends bright yellows, reds, and blues on his palate with another, thinner one. He splashes the colours on the canvas haphazardly. To his curious daughter, they look very appealing, but she cannot identify what he's painting. She cannot identify his paintings on most occasions.

'What do you think this is, love?' he asks her fondly after completing every picture.

She stands before the completed work, finger on her chin, wondering, and says the first thing that comes into her head.

'A cloud, daddy.'

'A snake, daddy.'

'Daddy, that's me!'

And each time, daddy chuckles and claps his hand, and says, 'Yes, you're right, my darling!'

She is squatting near her mother. Her mother is concentrating hard on the narrative she is supposed to conclude within the deadline she has set for herself. Her fidgety publishers have been hankering after her. Daddy has a hard time keeping them off the phone. There are never any calls for him; only for mummy. She knows daddy is waiting. Daddy has been waiting for years.

Her mother plays no favourites. She is a well recognised figure in the industry. She has already published two successful novels, and a handful of books on poetry which have brought her critical acclaim. She always shows her trophies to her daughter with unconcealed pride, running a loving finger over their titles. Many a time she reads out aloud from them, especially when daddy is at home. She has sensed daddy stiffen when she reads them … slowly, deliberately over and over again. Daddy has these passages by heart now. He purses his lips as she reads them again … and again. She blows away barely noticeable dust from their surface. She hopes that one day she would be an internationally celebrated figure.

The daughter is holding one of her mother's precious sheets in her hand. She is scribbling, or pretending to scribble, aping her busy and important mother. She lolls her tongue absentmindedly as she focuses on the task. Soon, she loses interest in her tedious work and turns the sheet over for more blank space. Not finding much scope, she begins to draw images upon her mother's neat writing. Suddenly, she turns in her mother's direction, staring at her uncertainly. Her mother is still too preoccupied to notice her, so she stands up steadily on her feet, picks up the rectangular sheet and toddles over to her.

'Yes, Shinu?' Her mother says, acknowledging her presence, but still not looking in her direction.

'Mummy, what's sex?' her little voice enquires ingenuously.

Her mother pauses in the middle of an important sentence she is writing. She warily turns towards her offspring.

'Where did you hear that word, child?' she asks a trifle sharply.

'It's here ... on this page,' says her daughter, exultantly waving the piece of paper from the manuscript her mother has been scribbling upon since morning. 'S—E—X. I can read it, see?'

Her mother instantly snaps the sheet away from her.

'Shireen, this paper is not meant for you! Don't be naughty and mess up my work! I've been working really hard since morning, and I don't want anyone to spoil it all. Now, go and play, and don't ask any more stupid questions!'

Baffled, little Shireen leaves her mother's side, perplexed little droplets rolling down her cheeks. Her unsteady feet ramble away from the room, her eyes still mistily focused on her mother. Suddenly, she feels herself being lifted by her father's brawny arms. He throws her up in the air, laughing, and catches her neatly as she descends ... squealing ... protesting ... laughing.

'Wazz the matter, sweetheart?' he asks after he's carefully brought her down on the ground again.

'Mummy will not tell me what *sex* means,' she complains to daddy. 'She scolded me so harshly when I asked.' Then, following a second's silence she says, 'Did I say something wrong, daddy?'

Her father guffaws again. 'No, darling' he says with a smile, 'you didn't say anything wrong. Mummy's been working too hard, so she's irritable. Never mind. You'll learn some things when you are older, all right?' He winks, and takes her little hand in his own. 'Come on, we'll go for an ice cream now. Mummy's been a bad girl, so we'll not take her with us, okay?'

His daughter sniggers.

'This is between you and I,' he winks, smiling.

She will never forget the taste of the vanilla softy that day. She spends the day with her daddy on the terrace, and they smear each other's noses and cheeks with oil whites, reds, and yellows, using fat and thin brushes, roaring with laughter.

Scene two. It is her eighth birthday. Mummy and daddy have been planning a grand party as usual. For some inexplicable reason, all is not well at home these days though life appears to be more than ordinary on the outside. Mummy smiles less often now. A couple of times, Shireen has caught her shedding silent tears all alone in secluded corners. She seldom sees mummy and daddy together. They are too busy with the hurly-burly of their own professional lives. Sometimes, she is intuitively aware of their gaze upon her, when, on one of those infrequent occasions, she enjoys the luxury of their company.

Shireen's classmates have recently finished a new chapter in the English class, 'Maggie Cuts her Hair'. In the story, a little girl called Maggie is exceptionally naughty, cuts her hair ziggy-zaggy all by herself, and gets into trouble with her mother and other relatives. For sometime now, Shireen has been feeling tempted to duplicate the daredevilry at home. Just fantasising about such a daring exploit enthralls her. She empathises with Maggie like she has never empathised with any character from a book. She yearns to read more, learn more about Maggie, the audacious heroine she fervently admires. She yearns to *be* Maggie.

The miscellaneous guests have arrived. She has just seen mummy, in her well starched new Dhaka cotton sari, rushing to the kitchen to bring the Black Forest cake daddy's brought from the best bakery in town, and candles—eight of them in all. She can see Kala trying to find the matchbox. There it is now ... the much awaited contingent of relatives at the entrance—the pretty aunties flaunting their latest buys, the stiff-upper-lipped uncles, her assorted and gangly cousins. All her friends and their parents, and bawling siblings, have arrived too. She smiles gleefully. It is time to make her grand entry.

She has copied Maggie to perfection. Her lovely long locks are gone, leaving behind a crop resembling some unidentifiable black mass a rapacious rat has feasted upon.

Her mother has just caught sight of her. She is more than horrified. The plate of boiled rice precariously placed on the table crashes to the floor, as she misses it completely. Shireen's act seems to have found its mark. The throng is roaring, rolling on the floorboard. The loudest amongst them is her daddy. He whistles and gives her a thumbs-up sign with undisguised mirth in his light brown eyes. She scurries to him, laughing, and father and daughter share a high-five moment.

The commotion manufactured by Maggie's disciple continues for some more time. Meanwhile, her mother is standing near the buffet table, clearing away the mess on the ground. There is an awkward, incomprehensible expression on her face. She keeps her feelings under wraps, however, and calls her daughter for the primary ceremony of the evening—cake cutting. The various guests are invited to assemble around the table. Shireen finds this reassuring. She walks up to the table, and takes her place, smiling at her mother, while her animated friends swarm around her. It's time. Everybody is waiting. Everybody is looking expectantly at the birthday girl. Her mother's eyes seem arctic … steady. And then, like a bolt her right hand flies out from the blue and lands a powerful whack on her daughter's stunned face.

Scene three. She is ten years old. A strange throbbing between her young thighs jerks her awake one morning. It is an indescribable sensation flouting expression, tearing her insides apart. And yet, it returns to her again and again every day. She cannot share it with her mummy or daddy. The sensation urges her to do strange, unspeakable things. She dreams weird dreams these days … of things tantalising and appalling. They return more and more often now, more and more persistent, unrelenting—like the blistering heat of summer. She must yield or she'll die.

Bobby is her best friend. He's a great guy with a whacky sense of humour and a contagious grin. He and his family are their distant neighbours. They live on a street somewhere behind their own. Bobby is a regular visitor to their house. He often takes her to an open field nearby where they carry little wicker baskets and dig out potatoes from the soil. It's a thrilling game. She loves playing in the mud. She loves playing with Bobby.

Today, she didn't want to go digging potatoes. Mummy has just walked into her bedroom looking for her. She can see her moving about through the little crack in the cupboard. Mummy wants her urgently for some work. She is calling her name again and again, annoyed … worried. She steps out of the room and her daughter can hear her name being called in the adjacent bedroom, bathroom, and the little balcony. Now she's back in her daughter's bedroom before Shireen has had time to step out of her hiding place. She feverishly prays mummy will not find her. But mummy is walking purposefully straight towards the crack now. Perhaps it's instinct that pushes her forward. She is almost there. Her daughter shuts her eyes tightly. Mummy clicks open the cupboard door easily, and stands gaping, as though affixed to the ground. Bobby and Shireen are huddled together on the shelf, their lower limbs stripped of any clothing.

Mummy and daddy are standing next to each other in her bedroom now. Mummy has already spent half an hour in his room, speaking in distressed whispers. Bobby and Shireen couldn't really hear anything except the rising and falling of tones. But they know that something significant was happening behind closed doors. Bobby and she have been rewrapped in their garments. Bobby is fretfully shuffling his feet. He refuses to look up. He hasn't been allowed to go home. Perhaps he's trying to hide his anxious tears. Neither of her parents has said a word though mummy seems more disconcerted than usual. She hasn't lambasted her today. She hasn't walloped her either.

Daddy is the only fresh arrival in her bedroom. He seems unperturbed as usual. Mummy drops herself on the bed. She is sniffing. Daddy makes no attempt to comfort her. Instead, he parks himself next to her on the bed, and looks enquiringly at his daughter.

'What happened, sweetheart?' he says gently, as usual.

His calm, unruffled voice has a miraculous effect on his daughter. She rushes to him with a fresh torrent of tears.

'We didn't do anything, daddy!' she cries, pleading. 'Honestly! I was just curious about the hard lump under his trousers, so I asked him to remove them.'

'You mean … he didn't persuade you to?' says her father, looking at Bobby. Daddy seems to be making a concerted effort to keep a solemn face.

'No, daddy,' she confesses softly. 'It wasn't Bobby's fault! I coaxed him into it. I told him to remove his trousers, and I removed mine on my own.'

'And what did you do?' her father asks intrigued, his face unreadable.

'Nothing,' she says simply.

'Are you sure?' His serene eyes look directly at her. He searches her face for guilt, for embarrassment. There is none.

She stares back straight at his unflustered face. 'I just touched him … there,' she says, 'and then mummy arrived.'

Is it pride that she reads on her father's face? She isn't sure.

'Very well, sweetheart,' says her daddy, turning his gaze towards mummy. 'You may go now. And never let mummy catch you like that again, okay?'

'All right, daddy,' she says, breathing normally again.

'A de-flowered virgin at ten!' her father chuckles, as his daughter makes a quick exit from the room with her relieved friend. 'I can't believe it!'

Her mother does not move. Her tears seem to have dried up from overuse. Only her eyes carry the colours of distress, of rage, of pulverised dignity, and degradation.

*****

Srikant, her lover, locked her in a python embrace again—their lips sealed, merciless, starving. His large, manly fingers stroked her wilful, spiralling locks, as her hard nails dug into his robust back, feeling the raw flesh, hungering for his musky, masculine body. He was inside her again…pushing his way urgently, impetuously into the deep ravine he passionately worshipped. Her thighs welcomed him, as they always did, bold and un-shy. They rolled on the bed together, he and she, implacable heat searing their souls, pushing their bodies into a rapturous boogie.

Wasn't this the pinnacle of experience, of fulfilment—the hysteria of divine worship? Wasn't this nirvana—the overwhelming, overpowering euphoria, the acme of ecstasy? Wasn't it true reverence—giving all, experiencing all—without holding back an atom of yourself? Wasn't this intoxication the ultimate quest of human life—of body and spirit, love and desire? Did one need more? Wasn't this the true celebration of life?

He stole a kiss, and released her.

'Things can be different,' he whispered in anguish. He truly wanted to believe what he said. 'We can be together—forever.'

She looked at him searchingly, studying his receding hairline, his Buddha-like calm face in silence. She had never seen a crease on that broad forehead. Even at this juncture of their lives, it spurned any turbulence. Yet, she was accustomed to reading the elusive tableau hidden under the tranquil surface. He made tremendous effort, but could not conceal his expressive eyes. And she read in those sorrowful windows, conflicting thoughts, choked emotions coughing and gasping for breath, and a masochistic submission to defeat.

'I know they won't let us,' he said, more resigned than angry.

'Who are *they*?' she asked, locking her slim, long fingers with his big, strong ones.

'They,' he repeated slowly. 'Our fathers, mothers, brothers, sisters, friends, foes, teachers, neighbours, priests, ministers, well wishers—the conscientious guardians of our society.'

'What guardians?' she spat, 'Guardians indeed ... who would smother us to death to save our lives?'

He shrugged.

'They are strong,' he said. 'Very strong.'

'And what about us?' she queried.

'Us?'

'You and I,' she said, putting her arms around his fleshly neck, his Adam's apple bobbing up and down. 'Don't we make the society? You and I, and others like us?'

He studied her childlike face as a teacher appraising a new student.

'You're so young,' he said, sighing. 'You and I, my love, are freaks, mavericks ... misfits perhaps.'

'And yet you ... and yet you want to?' she asked, surprising him, raising conflicting emotions in his mind again.

'Yes,' he admitted, pulling down the façade of strength. 'Yes,' he repeated. 'We can ... in a different universe if you like ... begin a new morn.'

'And don't *they* also say that your past catches up with you?' she enquired again thoughtfully, putting her elbow on her bed, and resting her head on her hand. 'Can we ever really run away? *Can* we?'

He stared at her. What wouldn't he give to be able to say yes? *Blind alley*.

He shoved her gently so that she fell flat on her back. Her luscious body lay exposed, Venus like, demanding him once more. Why couldn't they ever be satiated? Why did their inexorable desire broil them atom by atom, consuming their very essence? There was no peace, sleeping or waking. Desire was like a gaping black hole in the universe, remorselessly swallowing them moment by moment. He placed his luxuriantly shaggy torso upon her, taking in her perfumed soft-pillow skin. She unlocked her limbs flaunting the bald ebony-ivory triangle like a pitcher plant enticing its quarry. His wanton thirsting tongue glided from the youthful ripeness of her succulent twin mounds, to the irresistible navel, and lower, losing itself in the giddying vortex of passion.

'Stay,' he whispered, part beseeching, part demanding. 'Stay …'

*****

Scene four. She stepped into her troubled teens a year ago. She is now an attractive miniature, somewhat like a Chinese figurine. Her build oscillates between being plump and all right. She has better than average looks, and her shoulder-length thick mane curls naturally at her waist like giant waves whorling upon the ocean. But she is no ramp material. Most people believe her exquisite charm is her father's bequest. They would be correct in their assumption. She shares her father's looks, his temperament, and his passion for colour. She has her mother's fantastic power to cerebrate, and from her she has perhaps received a bibliophile's appetite for books.

Mummy and daddy. Mother and father. Man and woman. They sound natural enough co-ordinates in a schoolbook exercise on collocation. X and Y, XX and XY, yin and yang. She has experienced enough of life to understand that the situation at home is anything but idyllic. Her mother turned a non-writer three years ago, soon after an exceptionally stormy scene with daddy at home. That night, she knew, daddy had flung his best painting down the stairs in his fury. It had fallen face down into the gallery below, been ripped right in the middle, and spattered the floor.

No publishers hanker after her mother any longer. She is just another anonymous face in the faceless crowd. Her incomplete, unpublished manuscripts have been lying in stupor all these years, licking dust on her unemployed escritoire. The plastic covering is almost blind with thick stains. Nobody bothers to clean it now. Nobody bothers to enter her desolate room either.

She is sprawled on a mildewed couch, like a sickly animal in a filthy trench. Her used-to-be attractive features have also wilted as ripe *dasahri* mangoes lying neglected for a season. She seems to have fallen into the jaws of abysmal despair, and disrepair. Her head flops to one side, and the unkempt mass of black coconut skin sprouting from it covers her pale face, her gaunt hands hanging either side, corpselike.

The tea trolley placed by her side stands untouched. A motley collection of empty liquor bottles crowds the table in front. A half-full goblet still rests in front of her, already forgotten. She is too bleary-eyed to notice. Her sensibilities have yielded to an all-consuming inertia. Her mind is working like a washing machine dryer, desperately trying to hurl away the stains and smudges of total recall.

Memory, thinking power—distinguishing traits that outline the difference between mankind and the animal kingdom. Power to think, to reason, to understand, to remember: oh, what a blessing to be human! And oh, what a curse! What a curse to have the power to think, to reason, to understand, to remember! Just as well that her memory developed colander-like holes when it became impossible to take. Past and present slip through them intermittently, arbitrarily—retaining, discarding items from her life at will.

There's a cyclone inside her head—promiscuous images merging into each other—nauseating female perfumes, dazzling mascara, Gucci handbags, unfamiliar lingerie and evening dresses hanging in the washroom, high heels, and the flurry of shapely feet slipping and sliding into them successively. She is haunted by dissonant female voices giggling coquettishly from obscure corners, drunken laughter of her stranger husband—closing in faster and faster, encroaching upon her private space—the lone sanctuary in the world she considers home.

Shireen is standing in front of her mother as she groans, and makes a weak attempt to move. She knows it is one of those days. She would rather her mother stayed asleep. It is easier on her nerves that way. She dreads the frightening hysteria and temper tantrums that are as sure to return as the next morning sun. Her mother is not made of the same stuff as she. But defying her hopes, her mother's swollen eyes open, and close again.

'Go away,' she rasps. For some unfathomable reason, she cannot bear the sight of her youthful daughter any more.

Her daughter does not move. Too soon the door of the opposite room clicks open. Soft murmurs, seductive laughter, the sound of tusky heels tick-tocking unflinchingly across the mosaic floor into daddy's room. She waits for her mother's response. There is none. More sound—of clinking glasses, and jingling bracelets, of protesting aluminium rings being dragged across the heavy curtain rails. Pause. And then ... dim lights, music, and the shadow-dancing bodies across the mock screen. Shireen dreads another scene. The clock in her heart is ticking apprehensively. Any moment now. Any moment. But her mother's given in to deep slumber. An hour later, the door opposite clicks open once again. Low giggles, whispered goodbyes, and the familiar sound of those tusky heels fading slowly away. Her mother still seems asleep on the couch, her legs crossed, her forearm shielding her napping eyelids.

Scene five. Shireen is seventeen. The doctor's spacious, cold, square cabin has white plaster peeling off the walls. There are repulsive little damp patches like diseased sores on the ceiling, the new coat of paint fruitlessly seeking to veil them. There are two windows in the room, on either side. Heavy rust-shade curtains have been pulled and sloppily tied at the ends to permit some natural light to nudge its way through. The smell of isopropyl alcohol envelops the room, making it even more discomforting and austere. The Spartan extent has no reassuring face sitting at a receptionist's desk, no cheerful pictures hanging on the bare walls, no warm heaters shielding them from the biting chill. Even during daytime, it reflects the cheerlessness of the season.

Daddy stands stoically near the wrought iron chair, resembling a new school student in the principal's room. Daddy's eyes are almost wrinkled with weariness. His broad shoulders seem to slouch under the weight of his miseries. His usually neat and clean-shaven face sports an uncharacteristic, casual stubble. He seems to have put on weight. He seems to have put on age as well. In spite of all the haywire tailoring by time, his daughter believes he is still striking. He is standing uncertainly, staring out of the window on his right. There are a thousand questions swimming in his mind, but he maintains a balanced exterior.

Her eyes move to her mother standing close to daddy… taut, haughty, suspicious. She is wearing a loose shawl over a white polo-neck and old navy blue trousers, putting up a veneer of style and elegance. Her bloated eyelids and sallow features visibly indicating rack and ruin, however, shatter the pretence. She is standing with her hands together, fingers locked, trying hard to bar herself from trembling. Her shawl slides down her nervous shoulder and she quickly rewraps it around her neck, tighter this time. Her mistrusting eyes take in her surroundings skeptically. She wavers and takes a step back clutching her husband's hand.

'Why have you brought me here?' she enquires guardedly.

'Come... sit down here,' her husband replies gently, indicating the chair next to her.

'Where have you brought me?' She asks again, more loudly this time. 'This is not my sister's house.'

'Sit down, darling,' he says gently again. 'Don't worry. Nobody will touch you here. We'll just be here for a few minutes and proceed to your sister's, all right? Don't worry.'

'You are lying!' Mummy's voice is growing more vociferous. She has leapt up from the chair even before settling into it properly. 'You've been lying to me all along, haven't you? You are not taking me anywhere! You've brought me here to lock me up in this loony bin! You think I'm mad? I'm *crazy*, am I?'

'No, darling, no.' Daddy is up on his feet too, trying to quieten her. He pats her hand lightly, looking helplessly at the silent figure seated in front.

Her daughter steps forward to calm her, but her face instigates her mother further, and she jerks her hand away. The little pockmark on her daughter's brow is both an evidence and a reminder of what she has inflicted upon her.

'I'm not going anywhere!' She screams, glaring at the stranger still sitting peacefully in front. 'You can't lock me up, you bastard! Try and I'll send the police after you!'

'You are not mad, ma'am,' the gentle figure in front finally opens his mouth, and his calm, deep voice resonates in the bare room. 'Nobody is going to lock you up anywhere. This is not a loony bin, please rest assured. Your husband is an old friend of mine. I asked him to drop by when he told me he was taking his family to a relative's. I thought it would be nice to see all of you together. Do sit down.'

His mellow voice has a soothing effect. Mummy pauses, distrusting, then decides to settle down again.

'Can I offer you some tea … coffee?'

'And slip a sleeping pill into it?' Mummy is at her offensive best again. 'Do you think it's so easy to fool around with me?'

The psychiatrist is a well experienced exponent of his profession. Nothing her mother says seems to disconcert him. They stay in the room for more than two hours. The doctor skilfully reads his patient, meandering proficiently and discreetly into relevant details. Shireen and daddy listen, waiting, drawing comfort from each other's presence. Her mother fluctuates between stability and instability, lucidity and hysteria. It takes three brawny people besides daddy to overpower her when little signs of violence threaten to appear again.

The doctor has no option but to resort to tranquilisers. Shireen wonders whether her mother's fragile will has gone down on bended knees to narcotics. She hasn't the courage to enquire. Her mother stays in hospital for a week. Shireen and her father take turns to nurse the patient even at home. She resolutely refuses to acknowledge or hold any conversation with either of them. She has turned into a mute recluse, scribbling her muddled thoughts nonsensically on sheet upon sheet of blank paper, her unsteady hand mirroring the chaos within. Daddy and daughter work in mute tandem, exhausted and resigned, combating their own tormented souls in seclusion.

Scene six. Shireen is a glowing young lass of twenty. Daddy is standing on the terrace again, preoccupied with his easel. His unruly brush strokes spatter flaming colours on the canvas—scarlet lake, cadmium yellow, orange ochre, crimson lake. Who says her daddy doesn't belong to the same clique as Da Vinci or Mattice? There is a deftness she recognises in his work. A maelstrom of unspoken sentiments seeks unique expression.

This is daddy's final painting in a series he has been sweating upon for six months. The completed pieces in imposing Italian frames lie tidily piled along the terrace railing. Each seems to be an original masterpiece, yearning for a connoisseur's eye to applaud its genius. Daddy is moving his brush diligently upon the canvas. His dynamic, vigorous strokes seem to be making love to his canvas with complete abandon. He is painting the hues of mountain air, the freshness of a jungle cataract, the warmth of the January sun, the vastness of the cosmos, the freedom of spirit, the semantics of passion. Each stroke is a firm assertion of his brilliance.

The telephone rings. His daughter lopes across to the room to answer it. It is Mr Vyas. Daddy has been waiting for this call since yesterday. She is on the line for sixty restless seconds, listening. Her expression alters from anticipation and excitement to concern. She hangs up and turns to face her father. His face is indecipherable.

'That was Mr Vyas, daddy,' she tells him quietly. 'The exhibition's been called off. He said none of your paintings sold last time. Not one.'

Daddy continues to splash his painting with the colours of his soul. If the news has perturbed him, it does not show.

'I am sorry, daddy,' Shireen whispers.

There is an amused snicker from the study room. Mummy's hulking upholstery is reclining grossly on the easy chair, exposed to the eyes of the world. Giving in to her latest quirks, she seems to have renounced all decent attire, in the futile hope of winning back her once lover-husband; of driving him to her throbbing body once again. Her lubberly breasts droop obscenely like overripe fruit from a branch. Stratum upon stratum of fat deposit has turned her torso into a hideous mass. The bristly thatch between her vulgar and lumpy thighs is more repulsive than alluring. Patches of unchecked wiry crop colonise her thick neck and limbs. Her pitiable exhibition revolts him even more, pushing him further and further into abysmal gloom.

Mummy crosses her legs upon a whim. She props up a sheet of blank paper against a clipboard. She is drumming the armrest with her pen, pretending to write. But words will not come. Confusion has conquered her soul. She stares impassively at the sheet with a dyslexic inability to recognise the alphabet of life. Destiny is a dastardly traitor, deriding her flailing arms, and her gasping efforts to scramble back upon the sinking vessel of her life.

Daddy never raises any objection to her humiliating display, never makes an attempt to stop her. He is an unseeing, un-sensing assemblage of metal and wires in her presence. He has never displayed any inclination towards returning to her dismal assets. She is trying to repair the ever-widening chasm in their conjugal life with a needle and thread. Slowly, she seems to be abandoning the task. The motley collection of liquor bottles has suddenly re-materialised on her table. Dawn to dusk, she welters within the precincts of her four walls, sleeping, waking, sleeping, waking, till her soul cannot tell the difference any longer.

Father's friends come for a visit. Some return in his absence. She denies none. The postman comes, and the electrician, the neighbourhood grocer, and the computer repair man. Sunset after sunset she surrenders herself to the masochistic ritual. At some point she discovers she is about to be mother again. The little living, breathing seedling inside her womb infuses new verve into her. She decides she will have the child. Her husband continues to splash the canvas with vibrant, vivid hues of his imagination, displaying a callous indifference. Her daughter remains a mute bystander, watching and observing.

It is past midnight. Mummy wakes up to the violent pangs that have arrived without prior warning. She is rushed to hospital. The obstetrician is at her side, along with a fretting senior resident, and other sundry staff. The obstetrician carries out the final examination. All's well. Mummy is taken inside. Daddy and daughter dizzily slump on the fusty Rexene chairs in the waiting lounge, braving the biting chill in the night air. It is a nervous eight-hour wait in the empty antechamber. Each little footstep echoes in the corridors, trespassing upon the ears of sleepy relatives. Each whisper boomerangs amplified twice over. Time too is waiting… for the tomblike stillness of the night to break into a living, breathing day. A little bundle is born after a protracted labour, shrouded with blood and gelatinous vernix—mute and lifeless.

Six months have elapsed since the incident … six months since mummy was last heard uttering any sound, even a gasping slur, in front of them. She is just a ghost walking in the house. Once in a very rare while she wanders to the showcase, and lovingly dusts her ancient trophies with her scrawny fingers. Her heavy, fatigued body is still bare. But this is an unconscious bareness of an ascetic, rather than a vulgar display of a distracted consort.

It is late evening. They haven't found her. She was last seen running naked on the street by a bunch of street urchins who ran laughing, mocking after her in the pouring rain. They refrain from divulging her final halt, however. They say they do not know. Some say she ran towards the river. They never find her. They never find the body.

*****

He pulled her close. She let the heat of his hairy body douse her flesh and core, unabashedly. He caressed her submission and defiance gently, ingesting her essence one pint at a time, relishing each swig. His frayed soul dreaded the moment of release, not wishing to let go. He seemed to be hankering after something more … the invincible supremacy of passion, the overwhelming synaptic moment between twin souls, the euphoria of immortality—the knowledge of the absolute.

She pushed him away upon a whim, and he slid next to her, sighing, spent. She propped up her pillow on the bed rest opposite, and lounged herself against the padding, facing him. She flaunted her scrumptious form to his appreciative eyes. Suddenly, he heaved his sturdy body up and crawled to the side table. He pulled the drawer open and emerged with a delicate bag of blue velvet with silver strings. He dropped it into her eager hands. She sat up, smiling frivolously, animated as a child. She pulled the silver strings open gently, and dropped the multifarious adornments on the bed. She lay back breathing deeply, overwhelmed at the magnificence of her loot. He picked up the dainty gold chain and slipped it round her shapely neck, deferentially. She offered him her delicate wrists, and he slipped flawless gold elegance around each, inspiring her awe. Her long, smiling eyelashes wrenched his heart. He clad her little feet with pleasing anklets, tasseled her earlobes with spiral gold threads, bathing her youth in his lover's tender glance.

She slumped back to her position, ambling into the alcove of her mind, rummaging through the memories of that eventful night. Images flashed as a montage before her—harried feet running frenziedly this way and that in the unrelenting downpour, squelching across dirty little potholes; Hari, Gaurav, Roopa, Shiva—blurring faces pursuing probable eyewitnesses in dank corners, searching for mummy on byways and highways, in the brimming roadside ditches, and on derelict properties, calling, yelling, screaming their lungs sore.

She discovered Srikant that night, standing near the warm fireplace at three in the morning, drying his sopping wet clothes. She was drenched to the core—her wet hair loose, the chill rattling her aching bones.

As they stood together beside the warm glow of the fire, his gentle hand landed upon her shoulder. She turned her wan face towards him, and his arms locked her in a tight hug—caring and protective. She held on to him, allowing her smothered emotions to dash out. His love cradled her infant soul, siphoning strength into the rubble that she was. They stood clinging on to each other for an infinity. She stepped back, leaving the warmth of his heavy thorax. Then, in one vulnerable moment, he pulled her to himself, his importunate hands hauling, imploring her to return to him. She experienced a new sensation prodding her towards him now. Her inmost recesses instinctively responded to his maleness. The crimson flames beginning to devour her veins gradually yielded to the orange blaze raging within him.

She was shaken out of her reverie by her paramour's steady gaze studying her. A striking gold pendent lay on his robust metacarpals, with a thin gold chain dangling languorously from it. Almost instantly, her eyes were crystal bright. He smiled, rolling over to her, and lovingly placed the ornament upon the fire opal triangle between her thighs. His zealous hands industriously adorned the fire opal lips with tiny gold rings. She allowed his amorous fingers to flirt with the deep mouth of her gemstone, flooding her with a tidal wave of orgasmic ecstasy.

He sat back, letting her lie draped in the diaphanous treasure, admiring his handiwork.

'My masterpiece,' he whispered, smiling elatedly.

She returned his smile gleefully.

'You always understood, didn't you?' he spoke, his sonorous voice almost dissolving into a whisper again. 'You did…the only one who did…from the very first day.'

She moved over to him, wrapping his arm around her naked waist, saying nothing.

'Connect,' he said with a painful smile. 'Only connect … Man, did I connect with *any* woman in my life like—?'

Her arms slipped round his neck, and she clung on to him again. His arms in turn enveloped her gently once again, like the last, loving flap of a turtle dove's wings at dusk.

'I have to go,' she said, breaking free.

'Must you?' he breathed, resisting, obdurate.

'Yes …'

He released her quietly.

'I'm happy you carry my image in your womb,' he said, making a titanic effort to keep his voice even. His grief-stricken eyes sliced her heart into tender shards. He murmured, 'I would have given it my name.'

She looked at him frantically fighting back an emotional dysmenorrhea. 'You know it cannot be.'

'Cannot?'

'It mustn't,' she said, turning away. 'My mother … She wanted me to be a good girl, you know.'

'You will be … now …'

'Manav is a good boy,' she said. 'He'll take care of us, don't worry.'

Jerking herself up from the bed, she proceeded to clothe herself with renewed vigour, allowing him one long last minute to savour her nakedness for the final time.

He mournfully watched her hands gather her bric-a-brac, clothes, and books, little souvenirs of her fragrant presence in his life. Each little item, each tiny reminder was snatched cruelly away. Her task completed, she slung the leather bag on her shoulder, and wobbled towards the door.

'It can be different,' he choked, pleading like a terminally ill patient. He was aware that it was a vain effort to hang on to the shapeless mass that his life had become.

She partially turned from the door, her hand resting on the crescent-shaped door knob. Her tormented soul resurfaced in her eyes. She valiantly met his gaze one last time, and spoke with steely resolve. 'The wedding's on Monday ... at eight. Don't forget.'

He swallowed the asphyxiating lump in his throat, and nodded to her.

'Goodbye, daddy,' she said, clicking the door shut behind her.

*****

She lay on the four-poster bed, naked as a newborn babe, her withering velvet pansy skin daubing the air with a dizzying aroma, inviting ... egging him on. The weight of twenty-three summers seemed to have left behind indiscernible wrinkles on her body and mind. His artist eyes admiringly trailed the contours of her corporeal map, his ardent fingers playfully teasing the velvet cherries on her ample mounds. He was hard, ruthless, unsparing when he took her. She yielded to his thirsting tongue, and surrendered the crimson embers of her heart to the youthful brutal wildfire flaring within him. Spent, she slid limply by his side, thoughtfully studying his broad, Buddha-like forehead and serene eyes staring desirously at her.

Scene one. He is six years old. Mummy and daddy are sitting on wobbly, old wooden chairs across the stern-faced teacher at the table, dignified and cross-legged, speaking in hushed tones. He has not been allowed inside because the teacher informed him that the parent-teacher meeting is only for adults. He is standing outside the classroom with his ears pressed to the door. He doesn't want to miss what Mrs Guha has to tell his parents about him. In spite of the hushed tones, the voices ricochet to him as wayward echoes from the cold, empty classroom walls.

Mrs Guha is distressed. She cannot decide how to broach the subject. Daddy seems concerned.

Mew.

Mumble.

Hush!

Groan.

Squawk!

Mumble…

Whine.

'Indranil is really gifted, Mrs Pradhan,' the teacher's voice is almost apologetic. 'He is *brilliant*. And at the age of eight! Nobody will believe an eight-year old is capable of producing something like that. What luminous colours, what intensity! He's a prodigy, really.'

Mummy has a polite smiled plastered upon her face. She knows there is more to come. Daddy isn't too reassured either. He's shuffling his nervous feet.

'If he's so good, and you have everything nice to report about him, where does the problem lie?' says daddy.

There's a creaking sound of the teacher's chair being pushed away from the table, the familiar heavy *thup-thup* of Mrs Guha's big feet.

'Mr—Mrs Pradhan, I—it is true, whatever I've told you,' the teacher says awkwardly. 'I can say all that as an artist myself.' Pause. 'But now, I must talk as a teacher of this school. I can't have an eight-year-old student drawing nudes in my class all day long, no matter how brilliant he is!'

Stunned silence.

'That is all he draws,' says Mrs Guha. 'I told you he's brilliant, this boy … but I can't tell him that! It is just his good fortune that no other teacher has seen him at it so far. If the principal comes to know …

'You should get him an art teacher,' says Mrs Guha after a while. 'Give him formal training. Allow him to express his art uninhibitedly. But I can't do it for him here, Mrs Pradhan. I mean … this is still school, in spite of everything.'

Mrs Guha is looking helplessly at his parents. Daddy is as still as the rusty thumbnail on the display board. Mummy nods her head, understanding.

'I'm sorry to say this, but you have to do something about it without upsetting the child,' the harassed teacher says, resting her case. 'I hope you understand.'

Mummy perfunctorily nods her head again. His parents get up slowly to take leave. He quickly scuttles away from the crack in the classroom door.

They are walking towards the car now—Indranil, mummy, and daddy, in audible silence. Mummy is carrying his drawing book in her hand, hiding it underneath her coat, as though shielding it from the prying eyes of the world. Daddy will not look at him. He has never been so embarrassed. Mummy stops, oblivious of her husband. She is flipping tentatively through his drawing book, studying the flawless amorphous Ajanta Ellora Xeroxes breathing boldly back at her. She is mesmerised by the magnificent tones sprawled on the sheets: scarlet lake, cadmium yellow, orange ochre, crimson lake. She snaps the drawing book shut and calls him to her softly. She heaves him up with both arms. She says nothing, but holds him close.

Scene two. He is fourteen years old. He stares curiously at his tall, unclothed body reflected in the full-length mirror in the washroom. He takes his time admiring the resplendent thicket on his chest. He decides that those unruly, wiry threads sprouting on his chin, however, need shearing. He opens his mouth and lolls his pink tongue lecherously at himself. His hands fondly move to the bristly growth on the fleshy instrument between his thighs, working diligently. He attempted to shear his undergrowth last week as an experiment. The impulsive trial backfired though, and he spent a few painful nights suffering the bristly undergrowth creeping slowly back. He likes it as it is now.

He is re-running the incident in school that happened a week ago, in his mind. He remembers mummy and daddy sitting in the principal's room in uncomfortable silence in the afternoon, the black thunder expression on the headmaster's face; and the pained, cowering look on daddy's own.

Roar!

Cower.

Roar, roar!

Whine.

Roar! Snarl! Growl! Thunder!

Whine. Whimper. Groan.

'Can you blame me, Mr Pradhan?' The principal is coughing ire into his parent's stricken face. 'We run a decent school here, not a brothel! Our school may be small, but it is respectable. We have a reputation to maintain, do you understand me?'

Daddy nods mechanically, recoiling from the wrathful face hurling verbal mortar shells at him.

'A father at fourteen! Can you beat that? The media persons have made mincemeat of the reputation of our school now. The other parents are dangling swords at our throats, demanding rustication of this lascivious lout! Our name is mud.'

'But… but my son!' His shell shocked daddy utters in despair. 'If you expel him now, it'll be a stigma for life—an Albatross which he'll never be able to shake off!'

'Which is what he deserves, Mr Pradhan!' The unrelenting principal throws back at him. 'You should have checked him earlier. Now, the damage is done! Had it not been for that silly little devil he spurned, we would never even have come to know! And you say *sorry*?'

Trying to rein in his temper, he speaks coolly again. 'We have already dismissed the lady.'

Daddy looks imploringly at the school principal.

'Thirty-eight,' says the principal, returning his pleading look with igloo eyes. 'That lady is thirty-eight, Mr Pradhan, old enough to be his mother! Disgusting! He can't stay, I'm sorry. We are done with him.'

Mummy sits like a statue on the padded grey swivel chair. She is collecting the crumbling pieces of herself every moment. There is a haze in her head distorting the images in front of her. The buzzing continues inexorably within and without. Multiple cobra hoods suddenly materialise from nowhere, lashing their terrifying fangs at her. Déjà vu. She hasn't said a word to him about the incident. She will never say a word to him about the incident.

He returns to the present, his breathing coming in enthralled gusts, hard. He is getting drunk on myriad fusing images of feminine sweetness cuddling his aggressive phallus. There's a whirlpool of yearning let loose. His fingers work harder at his loins—taut, wet, aching. He gives in to the moment completely. A few minutes later, he stares into the mirror again—wet, palpitating, happy.

Scene three. He is seventeen years old. Mummy is sitting propped up on the bed in his parents' bedroom, painstakingly working at the chic metallic-blue laptop she has recently bought herself. Her industrious fingers are tapping away at the keyboard furiously. She often works at it when she is upset. Printed sheet upon printed sheet of her manuscript emerges from the bowels of the Laser printer perched upon a neat desk in the corner, buzzing gently. Once in a while it emits a tired wail. But mummy does not notice. She is too busy. Mummy has already published two non-fiction books, a couple of short stories, and an award-winning debut novel. She petulantly gets up from the bed to answer a phone call. It is her publisher. Yes, she is prepared for the book launch on Monday. Yes, her invitations have been sent out. Yes, her next manuscript will be completed this weekend. Yes, she will submit the compact disc along with the hard copy. She hangs up.

The doorbell rings. Daddy has just returned from office. He walks in with heavy, unhurried steps into the living room. Indranil is standing quietly at the other corner of the room, preoccupied with his easel. Daddy walks up to him, glancing over his shoulder at the austere abstraction on the canvas. He grunts skeptically, and proceeds to his unwelcoming bedroom. As soon as the door clicks shut, the austere abstraction is replaced by a vibrant nude: Venus in all her glory and grandeur—a breathtaking, lifelike piece—his passport to the best art college in the country. Daddy does not want him to go to an art college. He wants him to get some real education, to go out in the real world, and make some real money. He waves mummy away dismissively when she tries to intervene. She understands her son. Mummy is the only one who understands an artist's angst.

Of late, the raised voices from his parents' bedroom have been gaining frequency. Somehow or the other, every innocent conversation seems to culminate into a dreadful row. Mummy has firmly refused to be diverted this time. It is her life's dream that her son should get admission in the finest art college. He is a virtuoso. Daddy finds conversation with her increasingly tiresome. He finds everything increasingly tiresome. He feels like an outsider in her esoteric world of art and literature. He finds it impossible to connect with the accented English of her high-profile associates, with the glitz and glamour of the page-three horde she courts.

The raised voices are audible from his parents' bedroom all over again.

Hiss!

Rustle.

Slam!

Growl! Roar!

Sob.

Groan.

Hiss...! Lash! Lash! Lash!

'*My* son will not be a wretched idler!' Daddy is yelling in a familiar fit of temper.

'*Your* son?' Mummy is hissing venomously. '*Your* son such a gifted maestro? You must be *insane*! That's some arrogance indeed!'

Silence.

He cannot hear another sound. There is only silence... and the sound of more silence—loud, explosive. It's a silence that speaks volumes and writes tomes. It's a silence that will distort the ordinary face of their ordinary lives forever. It's a silence that each of them would be compelled to take in, chew, and swallow in the deep well of isolation, amidst heart-drilling sobs. It's a silence that will drown the remnants of pleasure and contentment in their lives. It's a splintering silence—a silence more clamorous than words, more killing than blade, more violent than rioting mobs—a heart wrenching, soul-raping silence.

The door of his parents' bedroom opens with a faint groan almost two hours following the last sound. More silence. Time has abruptly turned them into impromptu performers in a mime. A phantom in the shape of his daddy steps out, pushing the door shut behind him.

He does not know when daddy left the house...at least not the exact moment. He only knows that it was the same night as today exactly a year ago. It was the day when all the planets in the cosmos went berserk playing Bumping Cars, throwing his destiny out of gear forever. It changed the silhouette of his own life, wrote and overwrote mummy's. Mummy is an altered soul now. She does not write any more. She no longer entertains the accented English of her erstwhile high-profile associates; she no longer courts the page-three horde. She spends her days immured inside the four walls of her bedroom, sprawled on a mildewed couch, like a sickly animal in a filthy trench. A motley collection of empty liquor bottles crowds the table in front.

Once, only once, Indranil asks her, 'Mummy, who *is* my father?'

He receives no answer. Her mind is a gridlock suffering a deafening cacophony of warring automobile horns, driving her to lunacy. Finding it impossible to manoeuvre through the traffic jam of her life, she surrenders herself resignedly to the impasse. He is heartbroken at the picture in front of him. He parks himself near his mother, placing his hands upon her shoulders. His arms envelop her gently like the last, loving flap of a turtle dove's wings at dusk.

*****

The titillating smell of his cologned muscular frame cloaked her milky nakedness. His innate male aggression commanded her silken skin to submit to his thirsting flesh. She rolled over—resisting, teasing, goading him to come after her. He crawled over, aroused and enchanted by her voluptuous body. Her vulnerable yet ravishing face smiled seductively at him. He leaned on her back, deliberately crushing her soft-pillow flesh under his weight. She giggled. He longingly kissed her silvering curls, his warm, tender lips moving to the nape of her neck...

pausing, nourishing themselves upon the loveliness of her quasi-celestial femininity. She suddenly turned to him… burning, desirous, offering him the cozy plumpness of her bosom.

He succumbed to her with a passionate fever, gorging his tongue upon the delectable milky sweetness, his luxurious thorax massaging her smooth, dusky torso. She was Venus, Athene, Minerva, tantalising his youth, gulping his virility in hungry mouthfuls. He crawled to her, begging, beseeching. She permitted his fervent hands to explore the opulence of her figure, zealously venturing into her rich, sumptuous cave. He pressed her to himself, expertly kneading her gorgeous dorsal orbs, eliciting exhilarated moans. He flexed lower, his velvet tongue stroking her fire opal treasure like a fluid brush of an artist decanting brilliant hues of passion upon an expectant blank canvas. She melted, showering her physical bounty upon him. He returned her fervor with matchless oomph, carrying her into the nub of pleasure, barricading all other thoughts or sound. She hung on to him, latching her hard nails onto his flesh, inebriated with passion. She hit out at the multiple cobra hoods lashing their terrifying fangs at her; nursing her lacerated, desirous soul. He took her with the passion of the burning sun, making a valiant effort to scramble back upon the sinking vessel of his life.

Their interlocked bodies undulating in absolute accord, they burnt in the gluttonous fire of their desire, nibbling at sublime bliss for a long time. He released her. She lay next to him, reliving moments of unadulterated ecstasy.

Abruptly, he broke himself free. She watched him in silence as he rustled the crinkled sheets, rummaging through them for sartorial items carelessly discarded a while ago. She ran her index finger pensively over the ample skin cloaking her womb, staring vacantly in front of her. He sat down beside her, ran his finger around her navel, and pressed his palm lovingly against her lower abdomen. Time hung in the bedroom heavily like stale air, malodorous and stifling. He got up again, and donned his clothes quietly, not meeting her scrutinising gaze. Once dressed, he turned back to her, pulling the crinkled sheet away from her naked body once again.

'*Why*?' she said, pleading. 'Why?'

'Because I must,' he answered quietly.

'It can be different,' she said, choking.

He locked his big, manly fingers with her small, frail ones, and tenderly kissed her hand.

She looked at him, watching the setting sun.

'Don't worry,' he whispered, 'Lavinia will look after me. She's a great girl.'

Releasing her once again, he stood up on his feet, gathering his little personal items from the room, little mementos he might have left behind for her to hang on to and weep with. His task finished, he slung the deep blue denim bag over his shoulder, and headed towards the door.

'*Must* it be like this?' she croaked.

'It must be…It's a chance of a lifetime. Italy is a dreamer's paradise. My future beckons me,' he said, turning back from the open door, to meet her eyes. His voice was level, controlled. 'The plane leaves at seven, don't forget.'

She nodded.

'Indranil ...' she gave him a last yearning look.

'Goodbye mom,' he returned, and clicked the door shut behind him.

Naani

Naani. This dwarf of a word magically conjured up pictures of an old, wizened woman with silver spider weaves for hair, sprawled on a comfortable chaarpai. She would be telling *Panchatantra* tales to an entranced audience of young brats. Another naani would be a fragile woman with an untidy bun sprayed with grey, and a buttermilk complexion. She would be busily drying mango skin on old newspapers in the early summer sun, preparing for fresh pickles of the season. Yet another naani would have a toothless smile etched upon her walnut skin as she happily bathed her pigmy grandchild in the blue plastic tub every day. Naani: loving and affectionate, a magician, and a storyteller with an ever-packed repertoire—always an obliging bulwark against tyrannical parents.

Eleven-year-old Malashree pondered over this as she watched the nimble fingers of her maternal grandmother mechanically shelling peas at the dining table, her eyes glued to the saas-bahu soap on TV. Mrs Tiwary, a healthy septuagenarian, had the face of a fossilised non-pedigree cat, and a Hagrid body to complement it. Her walk heightened the effect, as the sharp clicking sound of her walking stick always preceded her entry into the room. Her eyes were omni-directional at all times, and the brows perpetually revved up with suspicion. In spite of her bulk, she had some majesty. Mrs Tiwary and her granddaughter shared as much love and warmth as did Saturn and the human race.

Mala silently studied her grandmother's chapped lips, a telltale dirty orange revealing years of unbridled addiction to betel juice and tobacco. She watched passively as her grandmother popped a few peas into her mouth once every two minutes, cleverly circumventing the ones that had any trace of errant worms. Mala wondered what would happen if, for once, her grandmother did swallow a worm by accident. A staunch advocate of vegetarianism, she permitted only her favourite servant to cook her meals. None of their other *filthy* servants was allowed to serve her, for she feared she would be defiled if they did.

Mala versus naani. It was perpetual war, and the chances of rapprochement were nil. Strangely, where the pleasing dell of love and fondness should have existed between the first and third generations of the same family, there had been a long, weary battle raging over the years instead. It had left behind only mutilated emotion and shambles of kinship.

Mala could not recall a time when her grandmother had behaved like a real naani, and held her lovingly, or smuggled chocolates into her palms, told her hilarious stories of her childhood, or done anything a naani did.

Having deferred from showing any naani-like qualities throughout her life, it was unlikely that she would develop any inclination towards them now.

Mala was born in spring, surrounded with adoring relations visiting from everywhere. As her only existing grandparents smiled into her face, Mala returned their affection with sporadic smiles and haughty princess frowns.

Being the eldest female family member, the task of deciding upon a suitable name for the new arrival had fallen upon Mrs Tiwary's shoulders. She pondered over various appealing options for three days—Malti, Meeta, Meenakshi, Madhulika, Meera, consulting one pandit one day and another the next and, finally, holding the babe to her bosom the third morning, announced to her expectant flock, 'She'll be named Malashree—Malashree Dwivedi ... my little Mala.'

Mrs Tiwary would massage little Mala, bathe her, dress her, and try teaching her rhymes. When Mala was old enough to go to play school, she would accompany her to school, and fetch her back at noon.

At the age of four, Mala caught pneumonia after a cold bath early in the morning. Though Mrs Dwivedi had insisted that her mother allow the little child to skip her bath that day, Mrs Tiwary had rubbished the idea, and gone ahead. From that time, Mrs Dwivedi gently transferred the child to her own care. When Mala and her grandmother together caught a stomach infection a few months later, the child demanded much precious time from her anxious parents. Mrs Tiwary, capable of weathering such teacup storms herself, was left more or less under the charge of their old and versatile maid, Veena.

When she got up from her sickness, Mrs Tiwary was found by her daughter in the kitchen one day, apparently very busy. These occasions were rare, for Mrs Tiwary didn't apply herself to a task in the kitchen unless it was for a very important person. Even her husband seldom got that honour.

'What are you doing, amma? You've been working hard since morning.'

'I'm making *kheer*,' replied Mrs Tiwary happily. 'You keep telling me I don't care for your little daughter.'

'Oh, amma,' her daughter squeezed her hand. 'That's so sweet of you. But honestly, you needn't bother. This child isn't fond of milk. She will not eat.'

'Nonsense! What child doesn't like *kheer*? She'll have it for sure! You just wait and see. It's my recipe, and I guarantee she'll love it.'

She spent her day labouring hard. She was tired and perspiring by the end of it all, but she was happy. She put the dish in a dainty little glass bowl, and sprinkled some crushed almonds for a topping. Then she waited for her grandchild to stroll in, and she did, eventually.

'There, there, my sweet, come here. Come to naani. See what delicious *kheer* she's made for you.'

Mala made a face.

'Come on, child,' said Mrs Tiwary, pulling the little girl to her.

'I don't want it!' Little Mala struggled in her grip.

'Shush!' Mrs Tiwary gave her a warning glance. Then, sensing that tears were quite close, she softened immediately. 'Come, come, sweetheart. Just taste this. It's good. I made it for you myself. Come... come... Taste it... There! Good girl!'

Being forced by an insistent grandmother to swallow a mouthful, the child suddenly choked and threw up. She tore herself free, and ran away from the room, whining after her mother.

It was always little things—a new dress bought, a little left-over something from the night before reserved for Mala instead of Mrs Tiwary, a TV channel changed for the little one's entertainment. But these incidents would linger in the grandmother's mind.

'It's not ar-goo-ment, naani, it's ar-gu-ment,' Mala, now a class-three student, laughed while doing her homework one day. 'Say that again—arg-*you*-ment.'

Mala mocked her naani as she could not speak proper English. She laughed because naani couldn't get her pronunciations right. And she laughed at her bookish usage of the language.

'All right, all right, *angrez*!' Naani hissed, cut to the quick. 'You go to a modern school where they teach you everything, don't you? Had I ever received that opportunity, I'd be speaking better English than you! I was born in the pre-Independence days when most women didn't even receive an education! Had it not been for my father, I would have simply wasted away in some corner. He educated me at home—taught me English, gave me classics to read.'

Mala tittered at the mention of classics. 'Wipe that ludicrous grin off your face, you little brat, or I'll break your legs!'

Later, guilt-ridden, Mala located an ancient copy of Dickens's *A Tale of Two Cities* in her library. She climbed on the wooden stool, and carefully pulled it out of the shelf with her clean, little hands. She blew the dust cloaking the cloth cover. Then she leisurely turned over the yellowing pages. Some of the printed words had fallen prey to starving insects. The sweet-smelling book held a strange appeal for the girl. The golden title embossed on its cover danced in the sunlight. Mala took it to the librarian and got it issued in her name for her grandmother's reading pleasure. Thrilled with her achievement, she carried it to her naani after school, and handed it to her.

'That's for you, naani,' she chirped.

'Hmm,' naani replied, running her fingers over the imprinted golden letters. The letters gleamed, like her eyes. 'Thank you, dear.'

'Read it. I have to return it to the library in two weeks. I'm sure you'll finish it by then,' Mala continued, pleased at her effort.

Two weeks passed faster than the first day of the New Year, and Mala was back, asking for the library book.

'What book? I returned it to you last week, Mala. I don't have it with me any more.'

Mala was confused.

'No, naani, I'm sure you didn't give it to me. You must have given it to someone else.'

'Now, why would I do that?' Naani fiddled with her walking stick, nonchalantly.

'Naani, please ... don't tease me.' Mala's heart-rate was accelerating every second. 'I need to return it to the library, or the teacher will punish me.'

'Come on, Mala, haven't I told you I returned it to you last week? What can I do if you are not careful with your things?'

She stood up, walked over to the mantelpiece, and began to wipe the dust off a wooden doll.

Mala was about to cry. She walked up to her mother tentatively.

'Ma … naani didn't return the book to me, I *swear*!'

'Shhh!' Mrs Dwivedi chided. 'You shouldn't swear, Mala.'

'Ma, please! Do something!'

'Oh, all right, I'll ask her. But if she says she's given the book back to you, she must have, Mala. Really, you ought to be more careful!'

Mrs Dwivedi called out to her mother and placed the question before her once again.

'Why does she ask me the same question again and again? Mrs Tiwary responded. 'Haven't I said I've given it back? Am I a liar?'

'No, amma. It's all right. Don't get upset.'

Turning to Mala, she said, 'You will just have to be brave and tell the teacher the truth, Mala.'

'The truth?' Mala's voice was a soft, small squeak.

'That you've lost the book,' her mother casually replied. 'Honestly! That's what has happened, isn't it? Just tell her that, and I'm sure everything will be okay.'

That afternoon, Mala knelt on the floor outside the library in full public view, wondering what kind of people committed murders. How couldn't one, with a naani like that?

Her resolve not to allow a free flow of tears broke only at home, past midnight, in bed. The missing copy of the English classic never made an appearance again. The episode was gradually forgotten by all, except Mala.

Despite her grandmother's rigours and regimented life, she had one weakness: a sweet tooth. The grand-dragon could not resist sweets, or chocolates, or ice creams, or any of those rich, creamy, fattening confections fresh from the neighbourhood patisserie.

Armed with this valuable knowledge, Mala had accompanied her parents to London the year before. Her grandmother stayed back home, claiming arthritis. Mala had breathed a relieved sigh. Perhaps she would bring back some chocolates for her. She was an old woman after all. Mala had forgiven her for the past, even if it took her a long time to do so.

And so a heterogeneous collection of boxes of Ferraro Roche, packets of Kitkat, Toblerone, Mars bars, and other rich, dark chocolates landed up in her grandmother's bedroom upon their return.

'Wow! For me?' Naani couldn't believe it. She beamed. 'Why, thank you, dear! How wonderful!'

However, that was the last time Mala saw that cache. Her naani hoarded them away safely in the little trunk under her bed. The family knew she gorged on one every evening after meals, but no one said a word.

Some days later, Mala was astonished when naani accosted her as she climbed down the steps from the first floor. The grand-dragon had been waiting near the balustrade downstairs for a while.

'*You*!' she bellowed, pointing her quivering finger towards her. 'You stole my dark chocolate last night, didn't you?'

'What!' Mala was flabbergasted.

'Don't tell lies, girl! I know it was you!'

Shock and disbelief were incused upon Mala's rather incredulous face.

'Naani, how could it be *me*? I was the one who brought the chocolates for you! Why would I want to steal them?'

'Then how could that Kitkat packet just disappear on its own? Someone must have done it!'

'Well, certainly not *me*!'

'Really, amma,' Mrs Dwivedi spoke up, appalled.

That evening, when Mala's father sauntered into the house from office, he could almost smell gunpowder in the air. His mother-in-law lay slumped on the sofa in one conspicuous corner, sobbing and sighing. He knew immediately that he must take control before the quirky wind could transform itself into a dangerous storm. So he squatted politely beside her while her tongue lashed his resigned ears.

Predictably, the night witnessed a closed-door session between Mala and her parents.

'But I *didn't* steal her chocolates, pa! Why would I?'

'I know, I know, but you know your naani, sweetheart. Go and apologise tomorrow, and give her some more chocolates. We'll buy you new ones, don't worry.'

'But pa, why should I apologise for something I didn't do? As for giving her more chocolates, I honestly have none left. I gave her all I had.'

'Well, buy some from your favourite corner shop then,' smiled her dad. He was tired of these battles now. The highlights of the day's match between India and New Zealand were about to begin, and he didn't want to miss that. 'Come on, be a good girl. Your pa needs rest now, so scuttle off!'

'Why doesn't naanu take her away to Chetan maamu's place?'

'Chetan maamu stays on the sea for six months at a time, Mala,' said her mother.

'But ma—'

'That's enough now. Don't be rude, beta. The matter's settled.'

'I'll kill her one of these days!' Mala screamed, as she slammed the door shut behind her. 'I'll kill her!'

Her parents looked at each other in silence.

Mrs Tiwary continued to scan every cranny of the house. She interrogated each servant thrice. She played a sleuth for the next two and a half days until, to her own embarrassment, she discovered the packet in the white party purse she had taken to Mrs Rana's house the evening the chocolates went missing.

****

Mala looked at the cuckoo clock on the wall once again. It was five minutes past five. Neeta, her closest friend, must have reached the neighbourhood patisserie already. She had ten minutes to get there. But she could not muster the courage to ask her mother's permission to leave as long as the grand-dragon was still smugly ensconced in her chair.

Finally, Mala made her way to her mother, with silent steps, and spoke to her in a deliberately low voice. Her mother responded in the affirmative, and Mala cheerfully scampered towards the door, only to be halted again. She found the grand-dragon blocking her path.

'And where are you off to now, madam?' The grand-dragon fired, drumming her nails on her walking stick, reminding Mala somewhat of Shere Khan.

'I'm going to meet Neeta at the patisserie. Ma's given me permission to go.'

The grand-dragon remained unimpressed by the imprimatur. A disdainful hiss followed from her. 'Neeta!' She spat. 'Anjali, you allow this girl to play and interact with that silly little chit in short skirts and noodle straps! Why, she's half nude all the time! That girl is a bad influence on this one! She ought to be whipped…going around displaying her body like that!'

'Amma, please,' Mrs Dwivedi said calmly. 'That girl is no more than eleven.'

'It's all your fault! It's because of women like you that our girls are getting spoilt, and going out of hand. No shame, no modesty any more. I will not allow it. Mala will not play with her!'

'Amma, be reasonable…please,' Mrs Dwivedi, afraid for her mother rather than of her, pleaded.

'Mala, go back into the room,' her naani ordered. 'Right now!'

'It was Neeta's birthday on the 21st!' Mala spoke, her voice rising. 'She phoned to invite me for the party. Naani took the call and told her sweetly I'd be there. And she never even informed me Neeta had called!'

'Really, dear?' Mrs Tiwary's honey-coated voice spoke in mock surprise. 'Must have slipped my mind.'

'Neeta didn't speak to me for a whole week after that. She said that I missed her birthday party on purpose! And now she would be waiting for me at the patisserie. When I don't turn up, she'll never speak to me again! Naani wants to rob me of my friends! She has never had a friend in her life! Everybody *hates* her!'

There was an imperceptible tautening of muscles on Mrs Tiwary's back.

'Now, now, Mala,' Mrs Dwivedi began.

'I hate you! I *hate* you!' Mala screamed, waving her arms wildly at her naani. 'I wish you were *dead*!'

'Mala!!!'

Mala rushed out of the room in tears, solemnly promising herself that she would dance on her naani's grave.

'Amma,' Mrs Dwivedi sighed in the awkward stillness after Mala had left. 'Now, look what you've done!'

'In our times, kids never dared to answer back!' Mrs Tiwary's voice quivered with anger, her hands firmly grasping her walking stick. 'They knew how to behave. This girl deserves to be thrashed!'

Mrs Dwivedi, realising that the situation was best left alone, retreated to her bedroom, without attempting to converse with her again.

In the cold silence of the living room, her elderly mother stood, her impassive face turned to the bay window, seeing, unseeing. Only the cauldron of her heart churned wildly—unseen, unheard.

Mrs Tiwary sat upon her bed for a long, long time, staring in front of her in the evening. It had taken her much thinking, and much resolve, to do what she was going to do. She was not a woman to be reviled. No, not again. Not after all these years. She would not believe it.

That night, her silent figure uncertainly walked down the staircase, with a packet of toffees clutched in her hands. She glided across the hall, and stopped at Mala's door, peeping in. There she was, the maharani, sprawled on her bed, with a book in her hands. Once every few minutes she would break into a loud guffaw. What a pretty little baby she had been. Had she ever thought she would grow up into this—this *vile* brat? Mala hated her naani, she knew. She hated her naani who had done so much for her ever since she had entered the world!

What a life of luxury they had led before her husband retired as a colonel! Had it not been for Anju's pregnancy, they would never have agreed to come and stay with her. And then she had persuaded them to stay on. How much she had had to cope up with all of a sudden. No respectable servants, no meals on time, nothing was ever in order! How she had hated it. She had hated every moment of her stay! And she had only just begun to take matters in hand when this brat entered their lives and—what hell broke loose!

Naani studied the smiling face inside the room. The longer she waited, the more she hated that smile—that exultant, self-assured, gloating smile always mocking her naani… those scornful eyes always catching her unawares, always contemptuous. Quite inexplicably, her resolve weakened.

'Amma, what are you doing here?' her daughter asked her in the hall a few minutes later.

'Nothing. I was thirsty and came down for a glass of water.'

'Oh, you should have rung the bell.'

'No problem. I didn't want to trouble anyone. I'm—I'm just going back.'

And she went back, the little packet of toffees still clutched in her hands.

That was three years ago, before Mala had attained womanhood; before the first casualty in her adult life occurred—an overwhelming crush—and the following heartbreak; before Neeta and she decided to part ways. The three years had witnessed much see-saw in their lives. At no point did the continuous battle seem to wane.

It was hardly fifteen minutes since Mala had finished her marathon session with history. She stood at the main gate, chatting with a couple of friends. There was a plump little girl with a dimpled chin, that her naani immediately recognised as the granddaughter of a prosperous neighbourhood businessman. There was a tall, lean boy with hair like overdone lasagna, whom she had snorted at in disgust the very first day she had seen him. And with them, another new face—a neater, pleasanter, more handsome face she was sure she hadn't seen earlier.

Mrs Tiwary had just finished the fifth and last round of Rummy with her friendly neighbour, Mrs Gokhale. There was still time before she left for the hospital with packed lunch for her ailing husband. After saying their usual goodbyes, she had ambled into the living room in search of the morning newspaper. Through the only floor-to-ceiling bay window in the living room, she could see the youngsters outside. If she leaned a bit further, her ears could catch snippets of the conversation as well.

Mrs Tiwary gathered that the new boy was called Roshan. That Lily girl said something about tennis practice, about some championship. And there was that other lasagna boy ... bleating, whimpering in front of Mala, silly fellow. Lily and he were making a frantic attempt to persuade Mala to play. Ah, so that was it. Roshan needed a partner for some mixed doubles. And what did that little chit say? *You cannot dream of finding a better partner than Mala. She*'s *amazing on court*. Bah! What sycophant friends the little shrew picked up! Why was Mala tentative? Something about naanu ... Practice timings ...

Could they be altered to suit her?

Sure.

Sure?

Absolutely.

Fantastic! Twelve noon?

Twelve noon.

Done.

There was a click-cluck-click of the walking stick, and Mrs Tiwary retreated from the living room. She needed to listen no longer.

The next morning, Mrs Tiwary was not up and about at her usual hour of 4.00 am. She was not even awake at 7.00, which would have been alarming except that when Mrs Dwivedi paid her room a visit, she could hear her mother's gentle snores even before she'd reached her door. So she smiled to herself and returned to her daily chores. Her mother was apparently in a holiday mood today, one of those occasions that occurred as rarely as solar-eclipses.

Mrs Tiwary eventually decided to quit her dreamland at 8.00 am. And then she pressed the bell coiled near the bed, for assistance. Kamal, the maid, instantly ran into her room. She was informed that Mrs Tiwary wanted her tea in bed. No doubt it was an unusual demand, but Mrs Tiwary's behaviour was in any case out of the ordinary today.

Her daughter decided to investigate. She stepped into her mother's neat little bedroom once again fifteen minutes later. Mrs Tiwary was slurping her tea slowly, relishing it. As she entered, Mrs Dwivedi realised with a sigh that her mother was in one of her 'moods' this morning.

'What's the matter, amma?' she said kindly. 'Did you catch a chill last night?'

Mrs Tiwary snorted her signature snort, but continued to munch her favourite butter cookies.

After a while she sighed, paused, and sighed yet again. 'Anjali, I'm an old woman. All my duties are done. My children are grown up and settled. I have lived long enough. It's time for me to go.'

'Why do you say that, amma? Who'll look after babu ji? And look at your sisters. They're even older than you and still going strong.'

'Oh, they have people to care for them,' Mrs Tiwary gurgled. 'Their children virtually dote upon them.'

'You mean we don't care about you?' asked Mrs Dwivedi, suppressing a smile, well aware how much the children of her aunts 'doted' upon their parents.

'Ah come, who cares about this lonely, old woman in this house? Now that my husband's in hospital, nobody bothers about me!'

'But amma, we're doing all we can.'

'For him, perhaps. What about me? Every day I have to travel three kilometres to the hospital to take him lunch. Oh, my back! It's killing. But who's bothered? Who has the time to relieve me of the task?'

'But amma, I thought you enjoyed the ride! Didn't you say only yesterday that you wished you could ride in the car morning *and* evening?'

Mrs Tiwary's wailing promptly grew even louder, and Mrs Dwivedi hastily retracted her steps.

'All right, all right. From today, you needn't go. Ram Prasad can go instead.'

'Ah, where does Ram Prasad have the time? I can't spare him. He does my betel leaves, he does my lunch, he does my plants. No, Ram Prasad can't go.'

'Oh, all right. Mala can go instead then. I know she spends some evenings there, but I'll speak to her,' Mrs Dwivedi promised.

Mrs Tiwary slithered back into her sheets to read.

At around 11.00 am, Mrs Dwivedi informed Mala about the altered arrangement. Her daughter looked like a batsman who's been bowled out at ninety nine.

'No! Ma, 12.00 pm?' she cried out in protest. 'Lily and Roshan especially changed the tennis practice schedule to suit my convenience! I'll completely lose face. Last time I missed the championship because of Chetan maamu's wedding! I can't do that again. Can't Ram Prasad go?'

'Mala beta, naani isn't feeling too well,' Mrs Dwivedi told her in her gentlest voice. 'No, Ram Prasad can't go. She needs him here to do her chores.'

'I just saw her watering her plants in her balcony, ma. She seemed perfectly fine. This is our only chance of winning the tournament, ma. Please don't do this.'

'Mala, don't be rude and selfish!' Mrs Dwivedi was on the brink of losing her usually well-maintained temper. 'Naanu's ill, and all you can think of is your tournament! You may not like your grandmother, but she is your grandmother. Besides, you never even think about your own mother!'

Mala had no ammunition against emotional blackmail. The obstinate latch of the rusty tiffin-carrier snapped shut with a loud creak. Mala made her way unhurriedly towards the door. Along with the meal she carried the shards of her dreams. Walking past her favourite patisserie (now an ice cream parlour as well), along the flower beds and two lush green lawns, should have elevated her spirits. It didn't.

She knocked the door tentatively and entered the patient's room. The temperature inside seemed a few degrees lower. The room itself was musty. Her naanu's shrivelled body lay on the bed, fast asleep. The young nurse reading his pulse smiled and nodded towards the petite relative. A little later, she left. Mala was now all alone in the dim, depressing room. She shivered in the requiem-like atmosphere. The relative's bed lay on one side, with bundles of dirty clothes scattered upon it. Mala pushed them to one corner and sat down in the empty space. She began to think. As the reflux of recent events began scrabbling inside her head again, she suddenly found her eyes tingling with tears.

The only time naanu opened his eyes in her presence, he called her to him. He held up his feeble hand, and stroked hers weakly. He whispered slowly, and with difficulty, 'She … she is like that … Don't worry, beta … You're a good girl. You'll be great one day.'

He slipped into unconsciousness once again. But Mala was grateful for his words. She had not bothered to camouflage her tears in front of her naanu, and she didn't feel guilty about them. Naanu was that one gem who had the perspicuity and sensitivity no other adult in her family displayed.

Slowly, Mala began to enjoy her visits. She preferred to walk rather than be driven to the hospital. She pulled back the soiled, heavy hospital curtains aside to allow cheery sunlight to pour into naanu's room. She discovered that her naanu's silent room was, in fact, a peaceful cloister that helped her concentrate better. She began to carry her textbooks with her to pass her time. Sometimes, when he was in a mood to sit up, she would read extracts from her textbook to him. He seemed to enjoy them greatly. He learnt, he taught, he laughed with her. She felt she would treasure these moments shared with naanu forever. The resentment at being forcibly sent to the hospital was already history.

At the end of the week, when Mala's father returned home from office, he discovered his mother-in-law ensconced on the sofa in front of the idiot box. She was dabbing her eyes with a grubby handkerchief. Though she hastily switched off the TV set as soon as Mr Dwivedi crossed the threshold, the dabbing continued intermittently. So did the muffled snuffles, in full view of her son-in-law.

Mr Dwivedi walked slowly to the dusty shoe-rack, and removed his shoes, taking his time. He had had a bad day at office. He could feel the first signs of migraine as he surrendered himself to the situation at hand. As a programmed automaton, he sat himself next to Mrs Tiwary and politely enquired after her health. Almost instantly, the floodgates opened and Mrs Tiwary drowned him in her tears.

'Who cares about this frail old woman sitting by herself all day long in this prison of a house? Does anyone ever ask about her? Does anyone ever take her out? No! Why, she isn't even allowed to visit her poor old ailing husband in hospital!'

'Why, amma? Who's stopped you from visiting the hospital?'

'Well, *Mala* takes him lunch in the day time, and *Mala* takes him dinner at night,' she sobbed. 'She goes there all the time, and doesn't even give her poor naani a chance to serve her dear husband in this crisis.'

Mala turned with incredulity emulsified upon her face. She had been clearing the dinner table in the adjoining room.

'Why, Mala?' She suddenly heard her father's tired and irritated voice speak. 'Why are you always quarreling with your naani? Why don't you let her take food to her husband if she wants to? Really, what's wrong with the two of you?'

A potent voice hissed deep inside Mala's heart. *Kill! Pick up the jug and smash her head with it!* The voice grew into a full-fledged thundering—bashing her brain, lashing her veins, blocking all other feelings and sensation. Her hands moved automatically. Her naani was watching her. Her fangs were still moving, though nothing she said registered any more. Mala's fingers pressed hard against the cold, heavy utensil on the table. Her muscles tensed.

Suddenly, she turned. 'Ma told me to go,' she told her dad, her voice steady. 'Naani *forced* her to make me go. I gave up my tennis practice sessions, my chance for this year's championship, *for her sake*!'

'Well, I didn't ask you to go every day, did I?'

'Enough!' Mr Dwivedi finally declared with authority. 'From tomorrow, amma, you can go in the day time. Mala, you can go at night, if you still want to, all right? That's the end of the matter.'

Hardly two days later, the family brought a withered but ambulant naanu back home. They had a quiet day. Serving and caring for naanu took most of their time. He needed much assistance even now, but Mala was pleased to be of use. For the moment, god *was* in his heaven, and everything was right with the world.

A few days after naanu returned home, naani developed a fresh hobby. One morning, Mala's deep slumber was interrupted at 4.00 in the morning by a blaring sound. Once she was better focused, Mala realised that the guttural and rasping screeches were actually supposed to be a bhajan. But naani's transistor was probably catching shortwave. The disturbance interfering with the waves was creating sheer acoustic rumpus.

Mala tossed and turned, trying to obstruct the noise somehow. She tried burying her head and ears in her pillow tightly, but that didn't work either. She felt the wrathful lava begin to boil and bubble inside her again. In a few more seconds, she could hear her naani's tuneless voice unsuccessfully trying to trill along with the bhajan.

This was exam time. The first day Mala chose to ignore it, thinking that perhaps naani's new whim was a one-off occurrence. However, it happened again the next day at exactly the same hour. Mala was rudely shaken awake once more by the disturbance from the wretched transistor. Naani had strategically placed it on the dining table to wake up the whole household.

The third day, a thoroughly harassed Mala approached her naani gingerly.

'But it's good to wake up early morning, and begin your day with the name of god upon your lips, beta.'

'Yes, naani, but I'm in the middle of exams, do you mind? I go to bed past two in the night!'

'Well, what can I do? Why don't you study in the daytime and go to bed at a decent hour?' Naani shrugged.

'Please, naani, have some mercy on me.'

'You should have mercy on your naani, girl! What entertainment do I have but this little transistor?'

'You can listen to it at a low volume, too, naani. Must you wake everybody up?'

'I can't hear anything at that volume; I'm hard of hearing, you know.'

'So you will not stop that morning noise, naani?'

'It's not noise, Mala; it's bhajan!'

'Right,' said Mala, gritting her teeth. 'The next time I hear it at 4.00 am, naani, believe me, I'll make your transistor vanish for good.'

Though stopped in her tracks for a moment, her naani continued her work, pretending to not to have heard her.

The very next morning, Mala's eyes mechanically opened at 4.00 am. She listened for the sound of naani's transistor, but there was sweet stillness in the atmosphere. Smiling to herself at the reprieve, she glided back into a dreamless sleep.

The exams had now begun in earnest. Mala was regularly burning the midnight oil, and burning it almost until dawn. On the morning of her math exam, as the clock struck 4.00, once again she was woken up by the most exasperating clamour from the transistor in the dining room.

It is impossible to barricade the flow of lava from the bubbling bowels of a volcano. And this morning, there was no stopping Mala. In five minutes, she was out of bed and back inside the sheets, and absolute silence followed. As the seconds-hand of the clock rapidly strutted across the dial, confused by the sudden hush, her naani turned up in the dining room. Her heart didn't just miss a beat; it stopped altogether when she realised that her precious transistor was gone.

Therefore, at 4.00 o' clock that morning, the Dwivedi household woke up to pandemonium. Mrs Tiwary's wailing brought the harried occupants of the house into the dining room immediately. Some wondered whether naanu had suddenly had a relapse again. But naanu himself arrived, nonplussed. Once she had everybody's attention, naani began to beat her chest and wail.

'Oh, my transistor! My transistor! That little scoundrel has robbed it, I know! She couldn't stand me listening to the melodious bhajans in the morning!'

'Who... what? What are you talking about, amma?' Mr Dwivedi was certainly not pleased.

'Why, *Mala*, that spoilt-rotten daughter of yours! She threatened me, that little rascal... and now she's done it!'

Mrs Tiwary poured out her woes once more, adding her own seasoning to the tale. As she finished, she detected Mala's tall frame standing like an alabaster statue at the door, listening quietly.

'There she is, that impudent devil!'

All curious eyes turned in her direction. Mala continued to stand in her place, her breathing deep and regular.

'Now, what is this, Mala?' Her pained father asked her. 'What is this I hear?'

Mala sighed, but chose to maintain perfect silence.

'Did you remove naani's transistor?'

'Yes.'

'Why?'

'Because I had no option.'

'Return it to her, Mala,' Mr Dwivedi ordered.

Silence.

'Did you hear me, Mala?'

'I'm sorry, but I will not.'

More silence.

'Look! See for yourself!' Naani pounced upon Mr Dwivedi triumphantly. 'Such an impertinent brat! Yes, yes, she can speak to her grandmother like that! But now? What will you do now, daddy? See how your daughter talks! That's what your modern education has brought.'

'Mala, return the transistor to your naani right now, and apologise to her!' Mr Dwivedi repeated in an assertive voice.

Mala met her father's stare with unblinking, unapologetic eyes.

'I will not return the transistor. I will not apologise to her either. I'm not sorry.'

Mala coolly held his gaze, her crystal eyes ablaze with wrath and challenge. The systemic hatred had slowly resurfaced, and he could sense some impending danger. He looked away and, without saying another word, walked out of the room, followed by a flummoxed mother-in-law.

'Hey, wait! How can you just walk away? Aren't you going to punish her? Has your love for your daughter made you so blind?' Mrs Tiwary spat after him.

But Mr Dwivedi was gone. His wife followed suit, and so did her own valetudinarian husband. Three years ago, she wouldn't have expected that girl to be capable of such a brazen act. But when she looked at her now, she saw another Mala—an independent woman, afraid of no one. And for the first time perhaps, she saw the face in front of her, with distinctly recognisable and rather familiar features on it—her own.

Time wove complex designs on life—of overwhelming, all-consuming passions; of constantly evolving relationships, of affluence and loss, of mistakes made and amends offered. Yet, when it came to Mala and naani, the pattern remained unaltered.

Soon after she finished school, Mala joined some art classes, and became enamoured with Pratyush, a classmate, who seemed to reciprocate her feelings.

'A boyfriend at the age of seventeen!' Naani was aghast. 'This is a very Western concept, Anju—this boyfriend-girlfriend business. It doesn't happen in our family.'

'It's all right, amma,' Mrs Dwivedi waved her aside. 'Pratyush seems to be a nice boy. We know his parents too.'

'Nice boy? Yes, you'll call him nice the day she lands up at home, pregnant. Nice boy indeed, trapping our girl like that!' Mrs Tiwary groaned picking the rice, for now it was difficult for her even to maintain a straight posture for long.

'Really, amma, you are too suspicious. The world has changed now. Anyway, you'll see him at dinner this Saturday.'

The Saturday dinner left Mrs Tiwary more horrified than ever.

'What kind of a boy is this—a boy with torn jeans and a ... *ponytail*! And not even a Brahmin. He's a Mehra!'

Mrs Dwivedi laughed.

'Don't judge a book by its jacket, amma. He's a great guy, and a wonderful singer. You'll love his music.'

At dinner, Mrs Tiwary sat next to Pratyush as though she had been made to sit next to a reeking little worm straight from a roadside drain. She scrutinised him through her thick-rimmed glasses. She wondered about his physical and mental hygiene. A man with abundant hair on the head and limbs, he seemed to belong to the lemur family. How could he be a classical music maestro—this man in a parrot green T-shirt, and jeans that looked like they hadn't seen a washing tub for months? A music maestro was the last thing he looked like. But he was supposedly one. Anjali had told her so.

He hadn't cared to shave. That didn't go down too well with naani either. When he opened his mouth to talk though, naani had to concede that he spoke faultless

English, and had impeccable manners. The nagging suspicion, however, remained.

After dinner, the boy began to sing. Mrs Tiwary, about to get up, sank into her chair again. She fixed her eyes upon him intently.

His deep, resonant voice hit the first notes with the perfect ease and confidence of a true vocalist. In the next few seconds, Mrs Tiwary found herself mesmerised. She stayed throughout the performance. He ended with a difficult *harkat* performed to perfection. Mr Dwivedi gasped. Everybody clapped. Naani was quiet.

His voice was an exceptional asset. And Pratyush used it well. He was on reality shows and giving live performances. He was catching many a famous eye. But Mrs Tiwary wasn't happy.

A week later when she spotted Pratyush at the gate yet again, she turned to her daughter and said, 'Really, Anjali, is he going to *marry* Mala? Never! That's what happens to all these famous people. They go corrupt. Why do you allow him to come here every day?'

'He's her boyfriend, amma. He comes home. He mixes with us. Isn't that nice?'

'But he doesn't allow her to study! That girl's just joined college, and she goes gallivanting with this fellow every day.'

'Relax, amma. She's doing fine. Look at all those trophies. You've heard how her professors praised her, yourself. Give her a break.'

'Bah, what do today's professors know! And last night Mala came home so late!'

'Last night, there was a party at his house. They were celebrating the prize he won at the inter-college music competition in the morning. I believe it was the best the college has ever had.'

'But—'

'And Mala wasn't alone, amma. Geeta and Pinku accompanied her home. His parents made sure she reached here safely.'

'I must speak to his parents,' Mrs Tiwary muttered under her breath. 'I don't like this. I don't like this at all.'

Pratyush's continued absence for over ten days made Mala's heart writhe for her paramour. She wondered what was keeping him away. Initially, his awkward silence on the phone had not bothered her much. But now, the distance seemed to be growing. She couldn't gauge the problem until, suddenly, an ugly little doubt began to claw at her grey cells.

And sure enough, when Mala entered the kitchen after college a day later, her flaming black eyes were enough to make Mrs Tiwary cower behind the granite slab where her chopping board lay. Her wrinkly, timorous fingers suddenly started chopping the cabbage with greater vigour, her eyes concentrating hard on the task.

'Oh, you're back!' Mrs Dwivedi smiled seeing her daughter.

'Why did you do it, naani?'

'Do what, child?' Mrs Dwivedi enquired, not unaware of the edge in her daughter's voice.

'Tell her, naani. Tell her what you did.'

'Why, what did she do?' Mrs Dwivedi looked up, puzzled.

'I didn't do anything,' Mrs Tiwary's tremulous voice answered. 'I did nothing wrong.'

'She almost ended my relationship with Pratyush!' Mala was full of fury. 'She went to visit Pratyush's mother behind my back and told her tall tales about him. *Him*! A pack of stupid, *spiteful* lies!'

'That chap was a threat to a young girl like you!' Mrs Tiwary snapped. 'Neither of your parents could see that, I don't know why. I had to stop him from ruining your life!'

'Ruining my life! *You* of all people thought you were shielding me?'

'He'll ditch you in the end,' naani warned her. 'Remember me then and cry.'

Had it not been for naani's age, and the umbilical chord binding her own mother to her, Mala didn't know what she would have done.

'I invented no tales,' Naani replied haughtily. 'I just did what your parents should have done.'

'*Why*?' Mala was exhausted. 'Why do you *always* have to throw spanner in the works, naani? Just why?'

Mrs Tiwary sat like an injured jaguar, her eyes twitching with anger. She refrained from answering.

'Were you ever young, naani?' Mala continued, bitterness dripping from her untamed tongue. 'I'm sure you were always incapable of love or romance!'

Naani did not respond immediately. She stared at the young face in front of her for a few minutes. Once again those features, those very familiar lineaments she had bequeathed, struck her gaze.

'Mala, I got married at sixteen. I have lived through war. I brought Chetan and Anju back from Rawalpindi during

Partition, all alone. Naanu was in the army. He had to stay on. I set up my house here from scratch. Those days, during those riots... when girls were getting raped everywhere, I had to keep my children safe. Through all that, do you think I had either time or inclination to *romance?*'

Her naani began to chronicle disquieting episodes from her life, but Mala was not listening. The story had taken another direction altogether, and Mala knew she had lost yet again. In a few seconds, she began to move out of the kitchen. She waited and watched, but the grand-dragon did not look at her again.

On her eighteenth birthday, Mala received her driving licence. It was an achievement to celebrate, given that neither her mother nor the grand-dragon shared the feat. Though Mala had feared stiff resistance from her grandmother over this, strangely, she created no roadblocks for her this time.

Today, it was Sunday. They had been invited to Mr Chatterjee's house for a Bengali dinner. Mrs Chatterjee was aware that naani had a fetish for handicraft and terracotta objects. She particularly wanted to showcase her latest treasures from a little village in Bengal. When Mala ambled into the living room, she could hear naani's voice speaking into the phone.

'Yes, Mrs Chatterjee, *of course* we'll come early... No, no, please don't bother about me. I'm not a fussy eater, you know... I'm eighty plus now—a fossil really. It's time for me to go... How much longer will I live?... No, Mrs Chatterjee, I really have no wish to live any longer (sigh)... I have seen enough of life... Yes, yes, come, you can speak to my daughter...'

Mala was about to leave in disgust, when her father's voice halted her train of thoughts. She turned around to face his slender structure walking towards her, looking a trifle anxious.

'Mala, beta, we have a little problem. Apparently, Reena aunty, your mother's old friend, has had a stroke.' He paused. 'We ... I mean, your mother and I, will have to go and visit her first.'

'Does that mean today's visit to the Chatterjees is off, pa?'

'Oh no, not at all. Mr Chatterjee's spent the whole day cooking for us! No, we can't call it off. But we have a little crisis then, don't we? And I think you can help us out.'

'What do you mean?' Mala smiled.

'You, my dear, must take our other car to the Chatterjees today.'

'Yipeeeeeeeeeeeee!'

'And you must take naani with you,' Mr Dwivedi added carefully. 'Naanu won't go, and we can't take her with us; it'll be too strenuous for her.'

Mala's enthusiasm suddenly plummeted to the ground.

'Come on, girlie; you can do it.'

'But pa—'

'Don't worry, naani will not bother you. I'll make sure of that, all right?'

Her father patted her head again as he led her to the living room, where he made the announcement to Mrs Tiwary. But she bolted like a wild horse immediately.

'Never! You must be out of your mind, son! She'll kill me for sure! No, no, I'm not going to ride with her! No way!'

Before she could stop herself, the sneering words were out of Mala's mouth.

'Why, are you afraid to die, naani? I thought you said you'd lived long enough! Weren't you telling Mrs Chatterjee just now that you wanted to die?'

Mr and Mrs Dwivedi were horrified at their daughter's impudence. Yet, she haughtily marched out before they could recover. Left with no option, Mr Dwivedi had to allow his morose mother-in-law to escort them in their car.

However, the lavish spread at the Chatterjees made the family forget everything else. It certainly lifted naani's spirits in a few palate-massaging minutes. By the time they were ready to leave, naani had forgotten recent history—that is, until fate did an about turn once again, and Mr Dwivedi found himself apologetically informing his mother-in-law that she would have to ride home with her granddaughter. Mrs Dwivedi and he had to drop two other of Mr Chatterjee's guests home.

The news settled upon Mrs Tiwary's spirits as a cold wave in December. No surprise that her granddaughter shared her sentiments. Mala got behind the wheel in perfect silence, and her naani clambered into the seat next to her, following her example. Mala adjusted the seat to fit her shapely legs into the narrow space. She kicked off the stylish stilettos from her feet and switched to flat shoes, ignoring her naani's snort. She took her time reversing the car from Mr Chatterjee's driveway, while naani kept her impatience strictly reined.

Once on the main road, Mala's eyes focused on the rearview mirror. Changing to a faster lane, she confidently steadied the car and jumped into fourth gear. They zigzagged through the hive of traffic at the crossing. Mrs Tiwary's dormant tongue slowly woke up once again. She began to do what any person not driving a vehicle should never do: side-seat driving. The tepid, staccato mumbling gradually changed into a more amplified whine. Mala still chose to ignore her. After twenty minutes of enduring her naani, she pulled over to the roadside.

'What are you doing now, Mala?' Naani demanded. 'Why've you stopped the car in the middle of nowhere? We aren't anywhere near home yet.'

'Naani,' Mala stretched her legs, not caring to look at her. 'I quit. Either let me drive in peace, or you can drive the car yourself.'

Naani was stumped. A decade ago, she would have stormed out of the car and taken a taxi home. Now, she felt too weak, too uncertain, too exhausted. There was no choice. She decided to maintain a glacial silence.

Mala revved up the car engine again. The next kilometre and a half witnessed a stubbornly quiet naani nursing her bruised ego. But then, a spanking new Toyota narrowly missed colliding with them. Mala's car abruptly plunged into a filthy pothole on the road, before re-emerging a few seconds later with a nasty cough.

Naani's ire resurfaced. 'Just look where you're going, *silly* girl!' she yelled, draping the sentence with the choicest abuses.

Kill! The same old voice knocked inside Mala's head. Uncoiling itself slowly, the feeling slinked forward, hissing—unhindered, unimpeded this time. *Kill!* The hiss grew louder, more insistent, lashing its fangs, clawing its way forward, till it had Mala by her throat, making her gasp for breath. This was the chance ... perhaps the moment she had been waiting for all her life. *Settle all scores once and for all.*

Mala could hear nothing else. Possessed, her predator eyes opaque with loathing, she pressed the accelerator with Herculean force. The car lunged forward, paralleling the speed of a missile. Naani was panicking. In the confusion of conflicting emotions, she found herself incapable of speech, and emitted a strangled sound. And then, almost as suddenly, she began to scream.

'Stop! Stop! Stop! Mala ... *Mala*, what the hell are you doing? *STOP!*'

But Mala was as deaf as a raging storm to a sinking ship on a wild, violent sea. Her relentless foot did not grant the accelerator a moment's respite. The car rocketed forward, now swerving left, now right for an eternity. Naani writhed in her seat, unalloyed terror ruling her vocal chords. The indistinct vehicles whizzed past her widow. So did the familiar buildings, and the Favourite Corner Restaurant (their erstwhile neighbourhood patisserie). They were going at a hundred and twenty miles an hour—rudely ignoring the potholes and speed breakers on the way. Naani screamed again, and again, and again. To Mala, each cry of terror was an antidote to the venomous voice devouring her insides, a balm to her exhausted soul. Each yelp of pain was a recompense for years of torture.

'Mala!' Naani's voice was hoarse—pleading, begging now. '*Stop! You'll kill us! Please stop! STOP! STOP!*'

There they were again—the pitiful yelps of a hapless mortal, the cries of a fallen monarch. Each sound was a palliative. It carried Mala to dizzying heights of ruthlessness. Adrenaline rush. Kinesis. Freedom. Mala was prancing in a world of her own—free. All the yesteryear stifling shackles had snapped open.

Suddenly, she was laughing like a lunatic. Then the storm died. Mala found herself being transported back, gently, slowly. Post climax, the tornado began to subside. There was the calm sea once again after the storm had passed, a post-coital stillness. Hush. Silence. As Mala slammed on the brakes of the car, there was a sudden jolt. The car swerved again, coughed a couple of times, heaving and shoving its occupants, and came to an abrupt halt.

Silence.

Mrs Tiwary sat as a sepulchral statue for ten minutes, her glazed eyes fixed on the windshield. Her mind was blurred. Somewhere along the way, she heard her daughter's voice saying, 'Come amma, take my arm. Come, get out of the car.'

She obediently emerged, trembling, fumbling with her walking stick. Then, with her stick clicking in front of her as on any ordinary day, she silently hobbled into the house.

Mala's naani never mentioned the incident to anybody. Early next morning, she announced that she wanted to leave for Chetan maamu's place immediately. Apparently, his wife was expecting again. Naani declared that it was her ardent desire to be there for the delivery of her third grandchild. Her near and dear ones might have been skeptical, but there were no other explanations offered, and none sought. The Dwivedis assumed it to be one of her occasional whims. Mala saw the luggage being loaded into the car outside the gate: two brand new Samsonite suitcases—a black and a dull grey, and incongruous with them, a familiar ancient trunk—naani's treasured wedding gift from her parents, standing as an outdated, outcast ancestor.

Naani never returned. She surrendered to her bed the day after enjoying the revelries at the birth of Chetan maamu's daughter. Mala had always waited for her grandmother's end during moments of wild fury and hostility. She had promised herself sleeping and waking that she would dance on the grand-dragon's grave. But now that the moment had actually arrived, she felt nothing but an inexplicable numbness.

Naani was dead before any of them reached Lucknow, her place of birth. It happened within a few moments. She didn't quit her hauteur even in death. Naani died all alone in her bedroom, in the absence of any relations and tears.

A few years later, sitting on a milestone somewhere on the narrow, winding roads in Nainital, Mala re-played her life with her naani all over again in her mind—cinemascope. She was playing with the ring, the slim golden band with an emerald leaf, Pratyush had lovingly slipped her finger through six months ago. He was now married to Karishma Pandit, Ustaad Prashant Pandit's beautiful daughter, who ran her own recording company. The wedding had happened yesterday. She pressed the ring in her other palm, hanging onto it.

From her shoulder bag, she extracted a packet wrapped in a flimsy white cloth. She unwrapped it to reveal her naani's ancient black transistor, the very gadget she had defiantly confiscated from her years ago when she was still an angry, young schoolgirl.

Mala pressed one end of the transistor to check for cells. It clicked open easily, revealing a rusty opening, the gooey brown liquid having left smudges on the walls. She roughly shook the object in her hand. The cells rolled out and fell at her feet before pausing, and rolling further down ... down, down, down ... hundreds of feet away from her. Mala was up on her feet again. She closed the little opening and, taking the transistor by its loop, hurled it forcefully at the snowcapped peaks in front as though hitting out at her creator. The little object flew out of her hand and, stopping short of its target by more than a few miles, struck a stray rock with a loud thud, and then, conquered, it changed its trajectory, and dived down ... down, down, down hundreds of feet below, and lay wrecked and derelict on the ground, having breathed its last.

Barkha Rani

She claimed she was a virtuous, god-fearing woman from a respectable Rajput family in Rajasthan. She remembered nostalgically the smell of the desert air, the sound of camel bells, the awe-inspiring citadels and palaces recounting history to the old and young decade after decade. She remembered young girls blithely pirouetting to deep-throated folk songs, flaunting the splendour of their multicoloured *ghaagra-choli*s; and the sequins and mirrors playing knots-and-crosses upon the latticework of rainbow colours on jackets and duvets. All these exhibited the best of Rajasthan, infusing life and vigour into the otherwise dry desert soil. And somewhere amongst those by lanes, she remembered her modest but impressive ancestral home.

'I never lifted a single finger to do any work in my parents' house in Rajasthan, what do you know! It would have been an affront to my father!' She boasted to all, vigorously rinsing an adamant stain on a milk container under the water gushing from the kitchen tap. Her tawdry red imitation georgette sari was pulled up to skirt length and gathered between her knees to avoid getting it wet in the dirty water. Her classic nasal twang enhanced the effect of her perpetual complaints flowing unhindered from her high-pitched vocal chords, making her voice sound grouchy and irritable even when she wasn't.

'I was my father's favourite little princess, the last of four sisters,' she continued, ignoring the rebounding water splattering mucky droplets on the pale yellow side wall, painting ghostly faces upon it. 'If he came to know I was working … and under such circumstances too … oh, Ram, Ram! All a game of destiny. I must have committed some sin in my previous birth. Otherwise, why would Mata Rani give me so much sorrow?'

It seemed she had been her father's favourite child, mollycoddled like royalty till she was given away to her husband at her wedding. She had apparently received some semblance of an education, but had forgotten whatever she had learnt.

'It has been so long! Believe me, I passed my class ten exams! I used to read Hindi books all the time at my parents' house! I loved to read. I could do math too. I used to maintain my father's financial records for him. I filled so many notebooks doing calculations for him meticulously. Honestly! I speak the truth. Now, where is the time to read or write? I have forgotten all I learnt. Life has changed everything.'

Her name was Barkha. She had an emaciated physique, and saucer-like vacant eyes staring out of basin-deep, sunken sockets. Whenever she was in a foul temper, the saucer-like eyes would develop a glazed coating over themselves; the sunken sockets would cave in a bit further, and give her face a malformed frog-like appearance. All day long, she sang her saga to stale or fresh sympathetic ears. She said she didn't really require employment; her family had enough to feed a dozen mouths, but she would rather not turn to them. She wanted to share her husband's burden, being an honourable and devoted Indian wife.

She just happened to be married to a drunken lout engaged as a fourth-class worker in a local factory, while she was employed as a cook for a middle-class family in east Delhi.

'Aunty, aren't you going to go to the mandir?' called out Leela, the young maid sweeping the floor. Barkha's nonstop complaints had hardly entered her disinterested ears. 'It's almost eight o' clock.'

'Arrey, Mata Rani!' exclaimed Barkha, peeping frantically at the clock and splashing some more water on the walls as she hastened back to her work. 'I didn't realise it was so late! Of course I'll get late for the aarti! Pandit ji will not be pleased. I'm supposed to be there on time to clean the floor. Oh, oh—that young vixen, Laajo, she'll be sucking up to pandit ji today since I'm not there… Ram, Ram, she'll get to ring the mandir bell also! And… oh no, oh no, she'll pick out all the best flowers from the offerings!'

She turned the tap off and spoke again, louder this time. 'Arrey, Leela! Just keep an eye on these milk containers for me, all right? I've put them on the gas stove to boil, but I really can't wait till they're done! I'm fasting today, you know… I'm so hungry… I've been constantly busy since four in the morning, but oh…I can't eat anything yet. There's no time, baba!'

'All right, aunty,' said Leela with a suppressed giggle as Barkha quickly set the sari gathered between her knees free. She brushed it, pulled her pallu over her head in a hurry, biting one end with her teeth. Then she waddled to the door with her *lota* and little puja *tokri*, knocking off a container lid in the course.

'Ram, Ram! Why do I have to upset everything just when I'm in such a hurry!'

She picked it up and reinstated the object in its rightful place. She was finally at the door two minutes later, and shut it with a loud bang behind her, still muttering garbled sentences to herself. Leela made no effort to decipher them. To her, this was an every day affair. 'Jai Mata Rani, Jai Mata Rani…mumble jumble.'

'Why doesn't she simply grab a bite of something between odd jobs?' said Mrs Dixit appearing in the dining room, and switching the television on with a bored face.

'She says she doesn't have the time, aunty,' said Leela, laughing.

'Rubbish!' Mrs Dixit laughed. 'There is enough time to take some tea with *barfi*.'

'Some people love drama,' said Shefali, her daughter, strolling into the room. 'Pseudo martyr!'

Leela broke into a loud though pleasant cackle. 'Oh, didi, last night Barkha aunty put water for tea to boil, and kept staring at it till it started boiling! She was chanting something…doing her *paath* as she made the tea.'

'Lo,' said Shefali. 'No wonder even a cup of coffee takes her an hour to make!'

'It's okay, beta,' said Mrs Dixit. 'Getting angry won't help. She only gets worse.'

Shefali helped herself to a Danish butter cookie from a large, white tin on the table. 'Sometimes I think she does it on purpose, just to wind me up.'

'Oh, come on. She is just a scatterbrain, that's all.'

Blissfully unaware of the conference in the Dixit dining room, Barkha waddled to the neighbourhood Durga temple. Her huge feet flip-flopped like Daisy Duck, in her electric blue Hawaii chappals. She zigzagged on the main road, as she usually did, thanks to her cataract-inflicted eyes. She was fortunate enough not to fall into any of the deceiving little potholes. Her sari swished and swashed, trying to keep pace with her legs. Soon she stood at the entrance of the temple, running an eye over the throng outside. The aarti seemed to have begun already. The enormous temple bells were reverberating inside the walls of the temple and outside. The sound of the *Gayatri Mantra* being chanted over and over by the priests added to the hallowed atmosphere.

Barkha took off her slippers and handed them to the keeper outside. Collecting the cardboard token from him to assure herself of reclaiming them when she returned, she washed her hands and feet. Then she quickly made her way inside, avoiding the pandit's eye. Her eyes scanned the vast space and found what she was looking for. A tiny figure, not more than four feet and a couple of inches tall, dressed in a threadbare sari, stood near the largest temple bell hanging next to the three marble steps which led to the main temple dais where all the deities rested. She was pulling the snakelike rope dangling from the mighty article to make it rumble. So lost was she in her task that she seemed to be on the brink of self-strangulation, the way she was pasted to it.

The sight of the young devotee swaying with the firm chord, her eyes tightly shut in prayer, made Barkha squirm. She resembled Meera lost in the bhakti of her Shyam. Barkha quickly made her way through the crowd to take her place next to the young woman. She handed her little puja *tokri* to pandit ji and shut her eyes even tighter, praying harder than ever. In a moment, her neighbour emerged from her trance and stared dreamily at her. Barkha returned her look with cold hauteur.

'You've been hanging to the bell all evening, Laajo,' said Barkha accusingly. 'Give it to me now.'

Laajo shook her head with a smirk, tightening her hold. 'I arrived earlier today, Barkha behen. You never give it to me when I'm late, do you? Today, I'll ring it to my heart's content.'

'Don't be mean, Laajo. I'm the one who does all the chores in this mandir. I have the first right to that bell.'

'Oh really? But you're wrong, Barkha behen. I do the same work for pandit ji, and I have as much right to this bell as you!'

At that very moment, pandit ji looked in their direction and gestured to Laajo. The instant Laajo detached herself from the giant object to walk over to him, Barkha grabbed its tail and clasped it to her chest. She began to sway with her eyes tightly shut just as Laajo had done, but popped an eye open every now and then to keep track of her archrival. And soon enough she saw her collect her prasad from pandit ji and retrace her steps towards her station. Barkha shut her eyes tightly again.

'Barkha behen,' said Laajo, tapping her shoulder as she stood next to her. 'Come on, you've had your turn. Now, move over and return the rope to me.'

Barkha still clung to the rope, deaf to her neighbour's appeal. She swayed with the rope left, right, and round, chanting Mata Rani's name. Laajo took a long breath. The next instant, she was at the puja *thaali* on the dais, culling out all the fresh and fragrant flowers from the devotees' offerings. She utilised the time well as Barkha's eyes were still tightly shut.

But suddenly surprised at the silence, Barkha popped an eye open again to investigate. She discovered, to her horror of course, that her neighbour had her puja *tokri* almost full of all the lovely flowers from the puja *thaali* on the platform.

'Hey you!' she almost screamed, rushing to the dais. 'How dare you keep all the freshest flowers! I want some of them!'

Laajo gave her a contemptuous look.

'Look at her! Just look at her, devotees of the mighty goddess! This woman saunters inside the temple halfway through the aarti, *demands* to ring the bell, grabs it by cunning; and now, when I've gathered nice flowers from the puja offerings, *demands* to have some!'

'Arrey! I come to the mandir and offer prayers day and night!' Barkha returned hotly, mortified at the hundred eyes glaring disdainfully at her. 'I wash the floor and clean the utensils, I ring the bell and gather the flowers every day, like a true devotee.'

'True devotee!' Laajo laughed in scorn. 'A harridan a true devotee, haha!'

A ripple of amused laughter flowed through the swarm. Barkha recoiled.

'Back off, or you'll be a victim to more humiliation, Barkha behen,' whispered a sympathetic voice from a trio of women standing behind her. Barkha turned, wavered for a second, and then obeyed. She quietly stuffed her puja *tokri* with some remainders from the *thaali* on the platform. Bowing before Mata Rani deferentially for the last time, she retreated, mouthing a thousand obscenities upon Laajo.

'But why do you quarrel with Laajo aunty, Barkha aunty?' Young Leela asked her later, genuinely amazed. 'How does it matter who rings that bell? And for that matter, what difference does it really make who collects the flowers from the offerings? They're just flowers.'

'Hush!' Barkha chided her with an air of superiority. 'It is for good luck, stupid girl! It's a chance to make one's voice reach the mighty goddess! And that conniving viper, Laajo…why, she isn't even the same caste as I! Being such a low-class woman, she tries to belittle *me* in front of the public! She thinks she's superior to me just because she can recite the English alphabet. As if that makes any difference! Bah!'

'Why?' Leela giggled. 'Then why do other people pray, aunty? If the temple bell is the only way to the ears of Mata Rani, then what about the people who don't even have one?'

'Shoo! This girl is too impudent!'

'And what about the flowers, aunty?' Leela enquired. 'Why are they so important?'

'Whoever collects the freshest flowers from the offerings persuades good fortune to visit her,' Barkha explained to her, picking the rice, sitting in the sunshine out in the courtyard.

'Aunty,' Young Leela twittered again. 'It's Karva Chauth in two days' time, isn't it? Are you going to celebrate?'

'Of course!' replied Barkha. 'Don't I always fast? Good you reminded me, because I still haven't bought my bangles. Oh Mata Rani . . . Jiji!' she called out to Mrs Dixit, turning her attention away from Leela. 'Jiji, I shan't come tomorrow. It's Karva Chauth time.'

'A Karva Chauth fast for that wastrel and wife beater?' said Mrs Dixit, aghast.

'Arrey, jiji, he's my husband.'

Nine days before the grand occasion of Diwali, the worthy women of the community gathered together outside their homes to begin their Karva Chauth celebrations. It was early morning, before the first rays of the sun touched the soil. They were dressed in their bridal gear, and festooned with jewellery: colourful bangles jingling on the wrists, with tiny gold discs winking from them; long earrings, heavy anklets, flashy nose rings and necklaces. Some obvious newly weds flaunted patterned *maang bindi*s enhancing the head and forehead. These drays of women assembled together to partake of their own potlis of *sargai* affectionately or grudgingly received from their mothers-in-law. An appetising smell of fruits, *aaloo sabzi*, and *puri*s filled the atmosphere. This would be their last meal till the moon was spotted late in the evening.

Barkha, too, formed a part of her own flock. She contributed towards the preparations of the puja for the day. A little wooden podium was especially hired from a nearby 'banquet hall' at a reasonable discount, following much bargaining. It was placed against the wall in a neighbour's courtyard. The ladies then installed the image of Goddess Parvati, Shiva's beloved consort, on the special platform. They knelt before it with closed eyes and folded hands one by one. All of them chanted their prayers in unison to ask the goddess for long lives for their husbands, and blessings for conjugal harmony. Barkha's voice rang the loudest among them.

After winding up the puja, she happily bathed the idol with rice and vermilion. Leaning humbly before her once again, Barkha mumbled something in low whispers. Sighing, she collected her puja *thaali* with the little earthen lamps burning upon it, and a pitcher of water precariously placed at a corner. Slowly, she waddled back to her house.

The moon, as it always did on the day of Karva Chauth, played Hide and Seek with the starving brides till almost nine o' clock in the evening. Upon its appearance, a thrilled voice excitedly announced the good news, and the wives impatiently rushed to their courtyards, verandahs, and terraces with their sieves and puja *thaali*s, bashfully calling out to their husbands to follow.

Standing patiently on her terrace, Barkha called out to her husband three times between regular pauses. He finally made an appearance, shuffling his annoyed feet.

She smiled. Then she picked up her puja *thaali* and the wire mesh she used to filter her flour, and bowed again before the moon. She offered water to it seven times. Then she placed the wire mesh between herself and her husband, and viewed his pockmarked face through it, still smiling coyly. She pulled the free end of her pallu tighter, bringing it over her head. Finally, she bent down to touch his feet. She now felt she had completed her duties as a wife.

As she bowed, her husband suddenly stepped back. His strong right foot flew at her, landing an excruciating kick upon her shocked face. She staggered and fell on the ground. The puja *thaali* went crashing against the floor, spilling all the water on the ground. The earthen lamps shattered into several pieces, their oil reserve sloppily spilt, and extinguished wicks scattered all over. After a few moments' pause, she wiped her bleeding nostril, and stared at the muck that now defaced the zigzag lines on her palm. She cursed, and wept at the filth that soiled her clothes and her life.

Her drunken husband roughly hauled her up before she had time to recover, and slapped her face.

'Stupid woman! Wasting money on this silly festival when she should be saving it! And she has the gall to tell me that I fritter money away on my drinking!'

Barkha stared at him, open mouthed.

'Take this, you bitch!' he said, hitting her mercilessly again. 'And this and this and this! You'll celebrate Karva Chauth, will you? I'll teach you to celebrate!'

The next day, she arrived at the Dixit household, much chastened, nursing her wounds with silent tears. She did not speak a word, but busied herself with the utensils. However, the telltale bruises on her face caught the attention of the occupants of the house soon enough, and an animated discussion followed, cursing the architect of her injuries.

'How dare he!' Shefali swore. 'How could you allow it, Barkha? That man must be a butcher!'

'He needs to be taught a lesson,' said Mrs Dixit.

'Honestly,' continued Shefali. 'He should have been taken to the police station and locked up for the night!'

'Oh Shefali di, that would have brought a bad name upon our family,' cried Barkha.

'What!' Shefali was incredulous.

'No, Shefali, di ... let it be,' Barkha pleaded, allowing her nose to run unimpeded.

'You should divorce this man! There are so many women's organisations these days. You could go anywhere; start a new life. Come on!'

Women's organisations. Hmm. Barkha had heard of those. The first time she had heard of one, she had been tempted to try her luck. And then she had come across Rukmani, a wretched widow from a nearby village, who had been intrepid enough to take such a step. Fate had lifted this desolate woman by her pelvic girdle, and dumped her at her in-laws' doorstep soon after. Some said she had been smuggled back by her offended male family members. Barkha didn't dare to recall what had happened next. Womanhood was murky business after your husband was dead, especially if you tried to be the strong, independent sort. Some did manage to reclaim their lives. Her own bua's daughter's elder bhabhi was one such admirable example. But then, that was her bua's daughter's elder bhabhi.

'No, di,' said Barkha, and gallons of tears flowed from her bloated eyes. 'I can't. It's not a part of our culture. I must—I must bear my burden. Mata Rani ... oh, why is she so cruel?'

Shefali reprimanded her. 'God only helps those who help themselves, Barkha.'

'Oh, let it be, Shefali,' Mrs Dixit intervened with a sigh. 'It's a matter of honour for some.'

Shefali gave up. Mrs Dixit retreated from the room quietly. Leela went back to wash the kitchen dustbin, listening with bemused ears, thinking about her own wedding looming at the horizon. Barkha returned to her dough with heavy steps, and a heavier heart. She turned the water tap on over the basin, ignoring the rebounding water splattering mucky droplets on the wall.

As the preparations for Diwali began in earnest, Barkha's episode was consigned to the background. There was much to be done. Diwali time meant a veritable bonanza for the family and servants alike. If the Dixits had had extraordinary fortune, it reflected in their buys that season. This period witnessed a sudden spurt of energy in every soul in the house.

Given her appetite for snooping, and good things in life, this season held a special charm for Barkha Rani. She wriggled out of her four walls at the sight of a new box of sweets or a gift pack, like an earthworm at the sight of rain. As always, as the spilling-over shopping bags, packets of *kaaju barfi*, *pateesa*, *dhodha*; Haldiram tins of *gulaab jamun* and *rasgulla*, assorted nuts, and other varieties of gilded baskets started trickling into the house, Barkha's eyes began to pop out. Every time an almirah opened in a bedroom, Barkha's saucer-eyes inexplicably materialised from nowhere. No matter how much care someone took, Barkha's snooping figure instantly appeared like an apparition, with a moronic grin upon her face. It began to get on Shefali's nerves.

'Ma, why don't we just give her her gift? She won't rest in peace until we do.'

'We will, dear,' replied Mrs Dixit, and immediately busied herself ripping open the new packet of burgundy earthen lamps. More such 'new' lamps were sought amongst last year's unused left-overs, and brought out. Silver paraffin candles especially sent by a cousin in England for the occasion were also brought out. Mrs Dixit and Shefali themselves prepared and put up the *kandeel* at the entrance of the house with the help of Barkha, Savitri aunty (their occasional helper), and Leela. Barkha inadvertently aped Montmorency to the T in the process. They spent a fine part of the day designing Ganesha *rangoli*s on either side of the main door, cheerfully soaking their hands in coloured powder.

The house was wreathed in a shaamiyana of yellow, pink, and purple lights cheerfully blinking from terrace to threshold. It seemed every house in the locality had a wedding that day. Finally, Shefali appeared with the gifts wrapped in butter-smooth, shining wrapping papers—blue, green, and mauve, and handed them by turns to Leela, Savitri aunty, and Barkha. Leela received hers shyly, quickly rubbing her soiled hands against her kurta before extending them towards Shefali. She opened her gift with great aplomb and squealed delightedly at the sight of an orange *lehenga choli*.

Savitri aunty was next. She seemed bowled over by her prize.

Barkha suddenly became too involved in scrubbing her utensils in the basin. She turned vaguely as Shefali approached her, and received her gift with pursed lips, examining the packet with a proctor-like frown. She opened her present to reveal a blue sari, the most beautiful of the lot, which Shefali had picked up especially for her.

'Hmph!' she said, unsmiling. 'Is that all?'

Shefali's grin disappeared instantly. 'Barkha, you are impossible!'

Mrs Dixit arrived on the scene with a disarming smile. 'Barkha,' she said, turning towards her sulky cook, 'Covetousness is the root of all evil.'

'No, jiji ... just look at Leela's gift! And such a bright colour too!'

'Tch tch, Barkha.'

'But jiji ... Mrs Sagar gives her maids a complete sari set every year.'

'Well, Barkha Rani, then you should go and work for Mrs Sagar.'

Her reply educed a snigger from Savitri aunty and Leela, enjoying the spicy scene, standing silently in the backdrop. Mrs Dixit left. Shefali, too, departed from the room in a dreadful temper. Barkha flinched, and hobbled out of the room haughtily, following her employers. Clutching her sari tightly she scowled, and left the other two fellow recruits whispering behind her back.

An ugly grimace decorated Barkha's face over the next few days. She was well aware that she had already blighted the festive mood on Diwali. But considering herself in the right, as always, she held her ground. All the house cleaning and pre-Diwali white-washing had thrown up several oddments and scraps of disparate items. As the post-Diwali excitement began to dwindle, Shefali began ridding herself of piles of junk. Every day Barkha began to see Leela exiting the house with a couple of bags of all sizes filled chock-a-block with miscellaneous articles. Once or twice Savitri aunty made an unexpected appearance, and left the house happily with more such bags. The sight of these bulging bags leaving the house in the hands of her rivals made Barkha's saucer-like eyes turn glazed again. Her envious squint enhanced the tadpole effect on her face. She kept muttering distractedly to herself.

'I'm an honourable woman. I never beg for anything. All the rascals get the best items in the house. I never get anything! Oh, Mata Rani! The person who works the most in this house never gets anything!'

As she mumbled, her trembling hands helped themselves to a tomato and two potatoes stealthily from the vegetable basket in the kitchen. She hurriedly tied them into a small *potli* hidden under the untidy folds of her sari, and continued her work.

As Shefali or Mrs Dixit crossed her path numerous times during the day, Barkha's crescendo suddenly rose, and the muttering acquired wailing proportions in their presence. Both mother and daughter, piqued after her dramatic performance on Diwali, simply ignored their eccentric cook. When, on the third day, Savitri aunty made her exit from the house loaded yet again with three enormously suspicious jute bags, it was beyond Barkha's endurance. From a slight, almost inaudible plaintive mumble, her voice rose ... and continued to rise, growing more and more belligerent every minute, to an obsessed lunatic's banshee cry hurling the choicest curses upon the flabbergasted guest and her progeny.

They all stood speechless, witnessing the spectacle, the devastating impact of Hurricane Barkha—Mr and Mrs Dixit, Shefali, Leela, and the remaining staff. Unbelievably enormous water balls fell from her glazed eyes. She continued to bawl for a long while, her skeletal frame trembling hysterically. Only when Savitri aunty had speedily dived out of the house, and onto the safety of her two-wheeler, did Barkha calm down. And once she had calmed down, Mr Dixit decided that it was time to intervene.

'What is the matter, Barkha?' he asked in a calm, quiet voice as Barkha stood in front of him, head bowed.

'Nothing, saab ji,' she croaked exaggeratedly. The snuffles tried to make a reappearance, but were checked by Mr Dixit's no-nonsense body language.

'If nothing's the matter, why did you make such a scene?'

'Mata Rani knows I'm an honourable, hardworking woman,' Barkha said, wiping her tears noisily, her froggy eyes stealing furtive glances at his wife and daughter. 'I don't beg for anything from anyone, saab ji. My family can feed a dozen mouths. I belong to a respectable Rajput family.'

'And this is how the respectable Rajput family behaves, is it?' Mr Dixit's voice grew dangerously quieter.

Barkha began to sob, and screeched stridently, 'All these rapscallions get everything from this house! I *never—*'

'Enough!' thundered Mr Dixit. 'Not a word more about this again, do you hear? Just give her one of those bags, Shefali, and let her buzz off *right now*.'

Shefali sighed, battling her indignation. She went into the courtyard and brought back three bags with her, bursting at the seams. She put them in front of Barkha.

Barkha's eager hands dived to the bottom of the bags, picking out objects, and examining them one by one. In a few minutes her face fell, and the familiar scowl returned. 'Why, this is junk!' she whined. 'You've given me junk!'

'Madam,' Shefali retorted, '*Of course* this is junk! What did you expect?'

From somewhere at the back, Leela snickered.

Shefali spoke again. 'Do you know what Leela took in that large bag yesterday? Broken pieces of porcelain! Gratefully too.'

Barkha sulkily withdrew to the washbasin in the kitchen, creating even more ruckus than usual with her pots and pans. Her face looked exactly like a poison dart frog's now. She kept bickering to herself, since there was nobody else. The grumbling sounds rose and fell whenever another servant fortuitously stepped into the hazardous vicinity. Therefore, most of them took special care not to enter Barkha's den unless there was dire emergency. Only young Leela continued to work beside her in silence.

Barkha determinedly refused to offer Savitri aunty any hospitality, or cater for her whenever she visited after that. She considered her a fellow co-worker, only a menial servant to the family like herself; so what if the Dixit family didn't? Over young Leela, she exerted her plenipotentiary powers. She claimed absolute proprietorship over her, and commanded her to do multiple tasks at the same time, not allowing her a moment's respite. Leela washed her utensils, especially the ones which had any trace of non-vegetarian fare upon them. Barkha always coerced her to do those.

'It's my Mata Rani fast today, you know,' Barkha would say to her adopted protégé.

'But aunty, you fasted only yesterday!'

'So what? It's *ashtami* today ... Just do those utensils, all right? I can't touch them today. I'll do them next time.'

It's Tuesday today ... It's a day before my fast ... It's a day after my fast ... Oh, I'm too tired today ... will you do them for me, Leela? I'll do them tomorrow myself, I promise ...

Leela washed the vessels, and she chopped the vegetables, and she boiled the milk, and she cooked the rice, and she made the *rotis*.

'I'm in a hurry, today, Leela ... Oh, Mata Rani, I'm getting late for the mandir again! Pandit ji will not be pleased. Just sauté those onions for me, Leela. I'll come back and do the rest.'

Leela usually did not complain. She genuinely enjoyed being employed and, as long as she could work in peace, she harboured no grievances against anybody. But today, she had been up since six in the morning, as her mother was suffering from a dyspeptic tummy. She had been flooded with domestic chores, and hadn't had time to grab breakfast before leaving home. A few hours of labour in the Dixit house had begun to trigger spasmodic cramps in her stomach. She suddenly realised how ravenous she was. After a little while she tentatively approached Shefali, and asked her if she could have a piece of bread.

'Oh, sure!' said Shefali, not thinking twice. 'In fact, you should have asked Barkha for it earlier!'

'But didi...'

'No buts! Where's Barkha?'

'Oh, Barkha aunty is about to leave for the mandir, didi.'

Shefali turned to the kitchen and yelled for Barkha. Barkha appeared, hurriedly adjusting her shawl over her sagging shoulders. She was dressed in a new satin sari. She was also wearing some jewellery and clumsy make-up, and looked prepared to step out.

'Where are you going, Barkha?' Shefali asked casually.

'Oh, to the mandir, didi. Today, there's a big *kirtan* there, you know. I don't want to miss it. A group of singers have come from another city especially for this occasion.'

'Well, Barkha, sure, you may go... but this girl here,' Shefali pointed towards Leela. 'She hasn't had a bite since morning. Just give her something to eat, and make her a cup of tea before you go, all right?'

Barkha visibly shrank from the task. She made no attempt to move.

'What happened?' asked Shefali, surprised.

'I can't give her food, didi,' Barkha said quietly.

'And why not?'

'Didi,' spoke Barkha, not looking in Leela's direction. 'Leela belongs to the sweeper class. She is an untouchable. How can I…?'

Shefali's jaws dropped wide open, and remained thus for almost sixty seconds. For any of the bizarrest reasons she may have expected from her cook, she certainly wasn't prepared for this. It took her some time to recover.

'Leela does half of your work. She does the washing, cutting and chopping and, sometimes, even the cooking for you! How is it that you don't remember her untouchability then, Barkha?' said Shefali, making an effort to keep her voice even.

Barkha pretended to be busy adjusting the pallu of her sari. She did not respond.

'I must say that is very selective *chooa-choot*,' Shefali poured out cynically. 'Go, you evil witch! I'll make her something myself. You needn't soil your delicate Rajputana hands!'

'No, didi,' Barkha stammered, hobbling into the kitchen immediately. 'I—that's not what I meant.' She fumbled with the gas lighter. 'Of course I'll make the tea. You needn't bother yourself, didi. I'm—'

'Just leave before I pick up the knife and chop you up!'

Barkha fled.

As soon as the door had slammed shut behind her, Leela's bubbling laughter erupted in the room. Her hilarity relaxed Shefali's muscles and, in a few minutes, she joined in too. Shefali delved deep into the kitchen's supply and lugged out some *samosa*s and *gulaab jamun*s. She microwaved them quickly, and handed them to Leela.

'Here, child, take this. And don't let that silly woman boss you around!'

Barkha did not turn up for work the next day, and the day after. She didn't turn up on the third day either, nor was there any news from her. It wasn't unusual amongst servants to do a disappearing act once in a while. But, on the fourth day, Mrs Dixit became agitated.

'Leela, I think we need to find out what's happened,' she said. 'If she keeps on absconding like this, we'll be in big trouble.'

Barkha arrived that afternoon, wearing a plain white sari, her limbs deprived of all the familiar gems and jewels. Her froggy eyes were brimming with tears. The familiar glazed look was very much in place. Mrs Dixit took one look at her devout cook and slumped right back into her low chair.

'What happened?' she asked, puzzled at the picture in front of her. 'All well, Barkha? Rakesh…?'

'Rakesh is fine!' Barkha almost snapped back.

'Oh!' Mrs Dixit stood up from her chair, nonplussed. 'Oh…Then why this widow's garb, and the tears? You gave me a shock just now.'

'Oh jiji! My daughter! My daughter, Bindu! She has run away from home!' lamented Barkha, plonking herself near her mistress's chair, like an Indian Rana Tigrina.

Huge water cannons burst forth from her eyes yet again. She wept, she sobbed, she wailed. She howled, she bawled, and she blubbered in front of her employer.

'Oh well, where has she gone?' enquired Shefali, a silent spectator so far.

'She has run away, didi—eloped—with that driver, Alok, at the Guptas' house where she used to work! That rascal deceived my daughter and persuaded her to elope with him!'

'Oh, come on, Bindu's no spring chicken. That girl's more than twenty! She has a mind of her own.'

'No, no, not twenty, didi!' said Barkha emphatically, sounding most injured. 'She's a child! She's barely fifteen! Honestly! I swear by Mata Rani. That villain took advantage of that and raped her.'

'Raped her!' gasped Mrs Dixit.

'Raped her!' gasped Shefali.

There were dismayed whispers from Leela and company.

Barkha sniffed. 'She was almost three months pregnant.'

'But she was staying with you,' said Mrs Dixit. 'Didn't she ever tell you?'

'Well, no. We didn't realise she was pregnant, and she never complained about that knave.'

'Three months ... and you didn't realise it?' Mrs Dixit was stumped.

'Well ... they used to meet regularly at the Gupta residence,' she said defensively again. 'How was I to know? I guess that's when the "affair" began.'

'Ah, so it wasn't really rape,' murmured Shefali. Barkha ignored her.

'But he got her pregnant!'

There were sympathetic sounds from the servants at the back.

'And now?' enquired Mrs Dixit.

'Apparently, they got married last night!' said Barkha, beginning to bawl again.

'*Arrey*, then what is the problem?' enquired Shefali. 'If he's married her, they're a couple now.'

'Oh, but that rascal—that rogue, Alok—he doesn't belong to our caste, jiji! He's the son of a *sweeper*!' She spat at the word. 'Oh Mata Rani, oh Mata Rani!'

'But how does it matter?' said Shefali. 'He loves her, obviously. And he has a regular job too. I can't see any problem, Barkha.'

'Oh didi! Bindu has brought a bad name upon our family!' cried Barkha, blowing her nose hard again into her pallu. 'We had already decided upon a suitable boy for her. True he wasn't literate. He couldn't calculate, or read the newspaper, but he was a real Rajput from Rajasthan!'

'All right, Barkha, all right,' said Mrs Dixit. 'She has made her choice, and she has gone away with her husband. And she seems to be happy.'

'Oh no, jiji!' exclaimed Barkha, horrified. 'We must bring her back!'

'What!' There was an astonished chorus from the Dixits.

'We must bring her back,' said Barkha firmly. 'Don't you understand? She has brought such shame upon the name of her ancestors! She has to come back, and abort that child! She has to obey her parents, marry the chosen groom for her, and make amendments for all the sins she has committed.'

'And now you will certainly kill her!' groaned Shefali, exasperated.

Barkha recoiled in front of Shefali's piercing gaze. Silently, she ambled to the kitchen, still sniffling and mumbling to herself.

'Aunty,' said Leela softly when they were alone in the kitchen. 'If Bindu didi is happy, why don't you let her be? At least her husband won't beat her.'

'Shut your mouth, you silly girl! You love talking through your hat, don't you? Now, don't meddle in affairs that don't concern you. Go! Go away!'

Leela retired to the living room, dusting the centre table and the delicate showpieces elegantly displayed on the ledge, while Barkha boisterously worked in the kitchen with her cauldrons, plates, and saucepans echoing the sentiments within.

A few weeks later Shefali was at home, thoroughly relishing the pleasures of a lazy weekend. She sat in the lawn waiting for Mrs Dixit, reading a novel she had recently bought. And then, to quench the craving for a cup of lovely *tulsi* and *elaichi* tea, she called out to Barkha.

'Oh sure, didi. I'll make a cup for myself too. It is getting cold now. I can't do without tea at least four times a day. You take it only once or twice, but I take it four times,' said Barkha, spouting a fountain of gobbledygook from her throat.

'Barkha, one teaspoon of sugar for me,' said Shefali sternly, dismissing her cook.

'Yes, didi, I take three teaspoons, so what? I have a sweet tooth. Everybody doesn't, right? No problem. I'll put in one teaspoon for you.'

Mumbling to herself again, she disappeared into the house. Shefali shook her head resignedly. Barkha waddled out into the lawn once again almost half an hour later with the much-awaited tea tray. She ceremoniously poured the tea in the new ceramic tea cups. Placing the cup on a saucer, she offered it to Shefali with quivering hands.

'Barkha, just what have you done?' roared Shefali suddenly.

'Why, didi, what happened?' A perplexed Barkha stared at her.

'Didn't I tell you to put in *one* teaspoon of sugar in my tea?' Shefali hollered, her temper mounting.

'Of course!' Barkha replied immediately. 'I did put in one teaspoon of sugar for you!'

'Then why's the tea so sickeningly sweet?'

'I don't know,' said Barkha, slipping into her storytelling mode again. 'Mine isn't. I mentioned to you, didn't I, that I take three teaspoons of sugar? So I put in one teaspoon of sugar for you and three for myself in the teapot.'

Shefali's hands mechanically reached her throbbing head, and tugged hard at her long hair from the scalp.

'What is wrong with you, Barkha?' she screamed. 'Yesterday, I asked you to put *kadhipatta* in the coconut *chutney*, and you put the whole tree in it! Day before, it was the salt in the *dal*. I've had enough!'

Mrs Dixit arrived just in time on the about-to-turn-unattractive scene, and calmed her daughter down.

'Yes, Barkha, you seem to be quite distracted these days,' she said. 'What's wrong?'

'Oh jiji, I need some days off,' said Barkha. 'You see, my mother-in-law has passed away. I really need to go to Jodhpur.'

Mrs Dixit helped herself to a cup of the discarded tea, and sat herself on a pretty cane chair, next to Shefali.

'But Barkha,' she said with a solemn face. 'Your mother-in-law passed away last year, as far as I can remember and, if I'm not mistaken, she passed away twice the year before that.'

Barkha shuffled her feet, and said awkwardly. '*Arrey nahin*, jiji. That was my *chachiya* saas—my husband's father's younger brother's wife. This time it's my own, my very own dear mother-in-law.'

'Barkha,' Mrs Dixit smiled charitably. 'Why don't you just tell us the truth?'

Barkha seemed to waver. Finally, she said, 'Jiji, we are getting our son married.'

'Mukesh?'

'Yes, jiji. He's old enough now, and he's started earning.'

'All right, so you want leave for the wedding,' sighed Mrs Dixit.

'Well jiji,' continued Barkha, suddenly becoming more garrulous. 'We went to see a prospective bride for him last week. But I didn't really like the girl much.'

'Why?' Shefali, curious as usual, ventured to ask.

'The girl was quite dark. She could read and write a bit, but what's the use of that? She wasn't fair like our son! I might have liked her better had she been fairer.'

'You were getting an educated girl!'

'But what's the point, didi? Our son can't read or write, can he?'

Shefali buried her face in her book.

A couple of days following Barkha's absence, Savitri aunty paid a visit to the Dixit house. Then she narrated the rest of the story.

'It wasn't just her son's wedding, jiji,' she said, rubbing her eager hands in merriment, and licking her lips. 'I heard the rumours, and I believe they may be true too! She brought her daughter back.'

'What!'

'Yes, jiji, they brought her back. I don't know how they managed it. Bindu and Alok hadn't returned to Delhi as far as I know, because they must have dreaded her parents' wrath. But Barkha's family found them anyway. One of her brothers—Barkha's brothers that is—was a notorious *daaku* in Chambal, did you know that?'

Mrs Dixit snorted, followed by Shefali.

'Seriously, jiji. Otherwise, how could they locate them so easily, *and* manage to bring Bindu back too?'

'What now?'

'I believe they are trying to get her divorced.'

Shefali groaned.

'It's a matter of pride,' said Savitri aunty. 'Barkha's trying to persuade her daughter to resort to an abortion.'

'Oh god!'

'That is why she needed the holiday,' continued Savitri aunty, pasturing upon the delight of her tale tattling. 'Believe me, jiji. No doctor from a standard hospital in the city will cooperate with her, so she has taken Bindu to a local *hakeem* in Jaipur for some *jhaad-phoonk*!'

There was a more amazed cry from Mrs Dixit, followed by a mild current of hmms and haas amongst the servants.

'Seriously jiji, I speak the truth,' Savitri aunty continued with a slurp. 'Ask anybody in her neighbourhood. They all know the story.'

Shefali tut-tutted.

Savitri aunty zestfully dug her teeth into the apple Leela offered her, and continued, 'So now she is forcing her to divorce him. She says she's defending her father's honour.'

'Wow,' cried Shefali. 'What an honourable family!'

Savitri aunty's attention, though, remained focused upon her large, luscious apple. She was quite pleased at the charged atmosphere her gossip repertoire had created. She finished her fruit slowly. The debate between the two Dixits regarding the whole affair ensued in her presence. She sided with neither party, but seized every opportunity to fling some sodium and potassium into the water.

Barkha turned up at the Dixits' doorstep again after four weeks, in the same old white sari. There was a mystifying absence of ornamentation, and despondence upon her face. Accompanying those were the familiar glassy eyes. She waddled in impassively, clutching her pallu in her hand, heading straight towards the kitchen, almost unconscious of the fact that she had been absent for a month.

'*Arrey*, Barkha!' said Mrs Dixit, noticing her all of a sudden. 'So you're back! How did the wedding go?'

'All right, jiji,' she gurgled inaudibly, her expression unreadable.

'I thought you'd be grinning from ear to ear after your son's wedding! What about some *mithaai* for us?'

'Oh, jiji,' Barkha was grouchy. 'Why talk of any *mithaai*? We got a Rajasthani girl all right, but she didn't bring much dowry with her. It was so disappointing. But what can one do? Mata Rani wished it that way. The wedding's happened now.'

'Better be a decent mother-in-law, Barkha, or you'll have the police at your door!' Shefali pitched in.

'Jai Mata Rani! Of course not, Shefali di! I can never torture anybody. I'm just a poor, honest, honourable old woman.'

This time it was Leela who filled in the missing details.

'Aunty, Bindu didi has run away again,' she whispered to the two lady Dixits the next day, in Barkha's absence.

'What!'

Leela nodded vigorously. 'Yes, it's true, didi. Bindu didi's husband came to fetch her, but her parents refused to let her budge from the house. He persuaded her to escape from her prison with her new bhabhi's help!'

'Gosh!' exclaimed Shefali, half laughing. 'I don't believe it.'

'Bindu didi's family is furious, aunty,' Leela grew more animated. 'Her father was screaming like a lunatic standing on the terrace last night. He must have been drunk. My brother heard him mouthing curses upon his daughter. They have disowned Bindu didi now—her father, Barkha aunty, everybody.'

Shefali smiled. 'I'm sure Bindu and her husband won't be coming back this time.'

Mrs Dixit sighed. 'No wonder Barkha wasn't excited about her son's wedding.'

'What about her pregnancy?'

Leela laughed. 'Apparently, Bindu didi created such a din at the *hakeem*'s that he asked Barkha aunty to disappear with her daughter immediately!'

The next day, Barkha was absent again. So was Leela. Shefali was frantic. Neither of the maids appeared all morning. In the afternoon, however, Leela turned up at the Dixit residence with some news.

'Barkha aunty is in hospital, didi.'

'Hospital? Why, what's happened to her?' enquired Mrs Dixit, having overheard young Leela.

'Her husband beat her up really badly.'

'Rakesh? Not again?'

'That's what happens when you celebrate Karva Chauth for such pathetic scoundrels!' said Shefali sourly.

'He came to know that Rambha, Mukesh bhaiya's wife, helped Bindu didi to run away. Nobody knows who told him. And did he get wild! God knows what would have happened if Barkha aunty hadn't stepped in front to shield her new daughter-in-law!'

'Oh gosh!' Shefali was amazed.

'Barkha shielded her daughter-in-law?' enquired Mrs Dixit.

'Oh yes, aunty! He picked up a broken liquor bottle to hit her. She fell, injured. There's a deep gash on her forehead. But that's what galvanised Barkha aunty into action. She ran to shield her daughter-in-law from further harm. Rakesh uncle was so infuriated that he kept hitting out at his wife relentlessly.'

'Didn't anybody intervene?'

'You know our set-up, aunty. Most of them just enjoy a scene in another's house. Finally, Mukesh bhaiya turned up, and chased his father out of the house. I think he's in police lock-up now. I don't think Mukesh bhaiya will allow him in ever again.'

'Oh, at last,' said Shefali, grinning. 'I guess that's the last of him Barkha will see.'

At the very height of the summer season, Barkha's familiar figure was spotted waddling again to the neighbourhood temple. Only the faintest outline of a scar remained on her brow, and an imperceptible deformity rested upon the bridge of her nose—the only reminders of the unhappy incident in the past. Her huge feet flip-flopped as usual in her favourite electric blue Hawaii chappals. Her sari swished and swashed merrily as usual. She carried her little puja *tokri* in one hand, loaded with fresh flowers for the offering. In the other hand she carried a neatly wrapped *mithaai* box.

Barkha took off her slippers at the entrance of the temple, and handed them to the smiling keeper. Collecting the token from him mechanically, she proceeded with the ritual of washing her hands and feet, and made her way quickly inside, smiling benignly at the munificent gods and goddesses looking down upon her.

'Jai Mata Rani,' she said softly, wiping her moist eyes with rose petals.

Her eyes scanned the crowd. Laajo's tiny figure, dressed in her customary ragged sari, stood near the mammoth temple bell, swaying with the dangling twisted rope. As always, she seemed hopelessly lost in prayer. But today,

Barkha didn't squirm at her sight. She did not rush to grab her archrival's place either. She looked on, smiling benignly, patiently waiting for her turn to make her offerings to Mata Rani.

Of course Rakesh had returned home. Not all the fetters in the world could have forced him to stay away. And he had returned to his antics. Once, drunk, he had insisted on painting their terrace railing blue, which had been painted red only ten days back in keeping with the hues of the house. He had insisted on re-painting it himself.

An ugly tantrum in the courtyard; a fragile ladder placed preciously against the terrace; a mad bull on the rampage. Perhaps Barkha was the only one who had sensed the danger. She was the first to see the beast—in time. She could have raised a warning cry. She never did.

Once she had offered her prayers and received the prasad, she offered her gratitude to pandit ji and made her way back to the Dixit house cheerfully.

'And what brilliant sunshine you carry with you, Barkha!' said Mrs Dixit beaming at her. 'So, what fresh tidings do you bring?'

'*Arrey*, jiji, Mata Rani has been so kind to us. Bindu's delivered a son!' an exultant Barkha exclaimed, opening the gilded *mithaai* box instantly, and passing the scrumptious *barfi*s around.

'*Arrey wah*! Congratulations!' said Shefali. 'We thought you had disowned your daughter.'

'How can you disown your own child, didi?' Barkha returned her smile. 'Now that she's delivered a son, all is forgiven and forgotten.'

'There, there,' said Shefali, shaking her head yet again.

Barkha laughed a genuine laugh in several years. The temple bells pleasantly echoed in the neighbourhood. A couple of street children gaily scampered across the kitchen window, chasing fire flies in the night. The warm summer breeze heaved a sigh of satisfaction, signalling to the moon to peep out.

Mrs Dixit made her way into the dining room, and switched the television on. Shefali hastily retired to her bedroom to respond to the shrieking telephone. Barkha cheerily waddled into the kitchen, and turned the basin tap on, the water gushing out energetically onto the untidy pile of plates and pans, and rebounding with greater vigour to splatter mucky droplets on the pale yellow side wall.

The Science Wizard

You ask me, you gentle citizens in Versace suits, Kanjivaram saris, and ten-grand footwear, why I do not log in to the World Wide Web. You ask me just why I do not care to register on any of these social networking sites ('Oh, there are so many!') that re-connect one so easily to one's past. You meet a lot of people there, you say. Old friends, people you've known.

Sure. It's easy. So easy. Walk into any Internet café, log on to the Net and lose yourself in the virtual world. Meet your past. Reconnect with ordinary, familiar faces and hold an ordinary conversation with them. Splutter some ordinary words that hang together to construct some ordinary meaning. Yes, it's easy for you out there, my ordinary friends, leading ordinary lives in ordinary circumstances, to ask me such a question. You flourish in the ordinary present scenario, and make megabucks in microseconds. You are busy in an ordinary pursuit—building an identity for yourselves in our fast-vaulting-forward world. Yes, you can enquire from an insignificant, disembodied voice from the abdomen of history until recently, in the course of an ordinary tête-à-tête, about his apparently ordinary existence (or the lack of it) in your real-virtual world.

The *web*. An interesting word. I'm caught in one too. But it isn't your far-flung World Wide Web on the PC. That would be ordinary. And ordinariness would be a luxury. I can't do ordinary things, for ordinariness is extraordinary to a senseless, shrivelled soul like mine. Faces—ordinary human faces—terrify me more than Black Death—hunting me, haunting me, in the drowsy hours of the eerie night and in the waking hours of the sun-swept day. Familiarity is the most heinous fiend, tugging at my conscience, wrecking my peaceful torpor. Ah, sweet blackout. Allow me, my dear ordinary friends, this comatose existence, for I have not the ordinary energy to carry on.

March 9, 1989

I dreamt a dream. I dreamt of becoming a rocket scientist. Mine was the world of fighter jet planes and MiG-29s, of Boeings and rocket launchers, of protons and electrons, of gravity and magnetism. I lived and I breathed science, especially physical science. It had the most amazing catalogue of secrets to offer. I could juggle with numbers as easily as I could juggle with chemical formulae. Others of my pack found it impossible to figure them out at the time. But the precise arrangement of letters and numbers flashed in my mind like the golden letters of the *Veda*s to the ancients. In a short enough time I was anointed as the *science wizard*, not just of my ordinary class, but of our ordinary school, in our ordinary little pocket in Delhi.

And so, a month prior to our annual exams, I had a happy father smiling down at a happy class teacher, standing inside the classroom, with his happy son in tow.

'Mr Joshi, you have nothing to worry about at all!' said Mr Datta. 'Uday is doing very well indeed. Even in his class tests he's scored more than ninety eight per cent in all his science subjects! I'm sure he'll stand first in class this time too. He's made it a habit now.'

Father glowed as though suddenly haloed.

'He's bound to become a rocket scientist someday, as he claims. He always scores a hundred in math, not a mark less!'

'Ah well,' said my incandescent parent feigning a frown, the pink, green, and blue gradients of the Aurora Borealis radiating from his face. 'I wish he would score a hundred in all of them.'

'Ah, come, come Mr Joshi, one shouldn't be so hard on the child,' smiled my teacher. 'If he but maintains his scorecard, he might get a scholarship to the best institutions in the United States tomorrow, you never know. Anything is possible nowadays. We don't know what destiny has in store for us, do we?'

'I hope it is good, whatever it is,' said my father, shaking my teacher's hand genially.

'Don't worry, Mr Joshi,' said Mr Datta, escorting us to the door. 'This boy is certainly destined for great things. I have no doubt about that at all.'

As we moved out of class, I could feel my pride puff up inside my ribcage. I agreed with my class teacher. I was destined for great things. Science was almost a mania, and I enjoyed being the best at it. At this juncture, I was neither acquainted with the spelling nor with the meaning of the word *ambition*. But I guess it was something that extended its claws naturally towards me. I took them with immense pleasure in my own hands, shaking them warmly. I loved the challenges ambition offered. It gave me a high to beat science at its own puzzling games. That is what they were after all—puzzles. Puzzles of increasing levels of complexity. And it was exhilarating to put the jigsaw pieces together to unveil the final unambiguous picture. It was easy. So easy. Life was just beginning, and I already had my destiny mapped out for myself.

Childhood is sweet, for it encourages you to believe. It is so easy to believe when you are young. It is so easy when the world around you hasn't started caving in to fuse the proverbial whites and blacks into foggy greys. It is so easy when you are still walking merrily on the red carpet, unthinking that the solid earth could be about to slip from under your feet. It's easy when you are still capable of holding on to prudent ideals; when you still have heroes in this world, and haven't discovered that their feet are built of worthless clay. It is easy when *conscience* has not been reduced to a mere difficult word printed in the dictionary.

Ah, perhaps I sound too misanthropic, my friends. But I speak the truth—the bare, unpalatable truth.

April 10, 1992

I was livid. Kaput, debarred, deposed. Stung, virulent, vindictive. Provoked, wrathful, rampageous. For once, somebody had managed to shove me a few rungs lower down the ladder in class, to usurp the crown of the new academic king. Bravo! The invincible had been vanquished—never mind if I was suffering from a bout of ill-timed chickenpox, never mind if my grey cells were too distracted to focus upon textbooks. It should have come to someone like me naturally, anyway, shouldn't it? I blamed none but myself. I competed with none but myself. Ankit Dave, the new sovereign (oh, but the masses love a new face!) was too much of a paltry mortal to trouble my self-esteem—that is, until she too went bonkers over the wretched flibbertigibbet.

Rashmi Sinha. With vital statistics deserving of a perfect ten, and features reminiscent of a Chinese doll, she was the hot favourite with all the men folk in class. She combed her Goldilocks curls tidily behind her ears, and spoke with a charming lisp. Anyone unaware of her accomplishments could easily mistake her for a primary school student. And yet, she cast a hypnotic spell on every y-chromosome juggernaut dawdling in the precincts. With my immaculate academic record, numerous awards, and enviable looks, I, a self-captioned Adonis, should have had no problem in creating an instant impression upon her soul. It never once occurred to me that a gloomy scenario could be possible.

Rashmi proved me really wide of the mark. With men of all shapes and sizes swooning over her feet east, west, north, south, and centre, she did not even notice my measly efforts at winning her attention. She was wont to be at her flirtatious best whenever I did catch her lovely eye. When fantasies of the extraterrestrial beauty began to pervade neutrons and photons, molecular masses and valencies, in my mind, I developed a niggling feeling that something needed to be done. I had no close friends, nor any patron to whose sympathetic ears I could unburden the new and so-far-foreign sorrows of my heart.

I spent a few restless weeks. Rashmi was a district-level quizzer and an athlete. What she wasn't at any level, however, was a scientist. She needed help. I answered her prayers in the form of an after-school science tutor. It would be so easy, I thought. But Rashmi proved me wrong once again. Where to me the complex theories and formulae came naturally and instantly, they were an affliction for my beloved. The simplest of them would have her eyes soaked. This was beyond comprehension to an enlightened entity like myself. I thought perhaps a little peppering of romance might help. But there was hardly any common ground from where I could begin. Rashmi was not interested in any Einsteins or Newtons of the world. She said she had never heard of Aryabhat or Sushruta, nor cared to hear about them now. She complained that I hadn't noticed her new haircut. I had no patience for these fiddly little useless things. Why did such an exquisite face acquire lambent dullness the moment she opened a physics textbook? I did not associate such miserable obtuseness with such loveliness. And I told her so in as many words. At that time, I was also unacquainted with the words *subtlety* and *tact*, and about what the lack of such precious knowledge could cost me.

The very next time I entered the classroom, I saw the pair of them sitting at her desk—Ankit and Rashmi. They were deeply absorbed in a long discussion about the mysteries of physics. But Ankit seemed to have enough patience for the whole forty five of us. He would simply repeat himself quietly, patiently, forty-five times over if she did not understand something. It devastated my pride to see him better me at the task. He was a whole foot and a half shorter than I, and probably a whole foot and a half plumper. He had neither ambition, nor poise. But in spite of such major handicaps, he seemed to have succeeded where I had wretchedly failed. His reserved and quiet manner appealed to the fairer sex much more than I, with my entire curriculum vitae, ever did. He recaptured my tiara following our annual exams that year. Worse, I caught the new love-struck couple clandestinely lip-locked in a particularly deserted corner of the school on a particularly bad day.

'Cuckold!' whispered a nasty voice in my pink, hot ear as I passed the infamous trio of my class. Gautam Sahni, Karan Bajaj, and Raghav Shinde—the three worthy heirs of Lucifer, were lurking infuriatingly in the very same corridor at the very same time. Gautam belonged to one of the most affluent families in the city—the legendary Sahnis—the fifth or sixth largest liquor barons in the country. He was humongous, and always draped in the finest foreign brands. At fourteen, he drove the fanciest sedans to school, forcing his chauffeur into the back seat. His father was a bigwig in the city circles, and had some strong political leanings. He knew the right noble patricians in the right places. So it made Gautam quite secure against our feeble school laws. Karan and Raghav did not belong to such influential families, but must have surely been born with a couple of silver spoons stuffed into their big mouths. They were yes men to their reckless boss, the humble sidekicks to the big mahout. And they had a bellyful of horror stories to their credit. No student in his right mind ever crossed the path of the Terrible Trio.

'What? What did you say?' I said, growing quite red.

'Cuckold!' said Gautam, the principal leader, with a dirty smirk.

'What's that?' I asked guardedly, suddenly annoyed at my own question.

The trio burst into a malicious guffaw.

'Cuckold, idiot!' said Raghav. 'Don't you even know what *that* means?'

'Nope,' I admitted simply, and kicked myself again for needlessly prolonging the conversation.

'A man whose wife has run away with another man is called a cuckold,' recited Karan in a shrill voice. His fellow rascals chuckled.

'I'm no cuckold,' I said, more vehement than I wanted to sound. 'I'm not married to her!'

'Oh really?' said Gautam in a sickly sweet voice. 'We thought you were—almost!'

More guffawing and catcalls followed.

'She called you arrogant,' tittered Karan. 'An arrogant and opinionated fool!'

Their cold-blooded comments cut through me like a sharp scythe, slashing my pride. It wasn't my heart their callous remarks wounded, for I was sure I was not really in love with her. But I could not forgive Ankit for beating me at it. More than that, it was the grave crime of dethroning me from the first position in class, that I could not disregard. It was defeat I abhorred.

'Well, whiz kid,' said Gautam, addressing me in a patronising tone. I stared at him, still silent. 'We ought to do something about that silly traitor, oughtn't we?'

I looked at him, he looked at me. He winked, with a broad smile exposing his tinted teeth.

'What do you mean?' I asked him, not sure what he was getting at. He languidly walked over to me, and offered his yellow smile again.

'A deal,' he said.

'I am sorry, I don't understand.'

'That puny Ankit Dave,' he said, as his right hand dived into his pocket and reappeared with a cigarette and an imported lighter. I didn't know he also smoked. The surprise on my face must have tickled him, for he cheerfully smiled again, and lit his cigarette attempting a deplorable imitation of Rajnikant.

'He's been making a nuisance of himself, hasn't he?'

The humble sidekicks gurgled mirthlessly.

'Well,' I said defensively. 'I was ill this time ... and he was just lucky. Besides, both the science models that made it to the state level were mine.'

The trio laughed again. It defied my intelligence what they found so hilarious all the time.

'We'll get rid of him for you,' said Gautam seriously. I drew back in perfect horror. He smiled again. 'Don't worry,' he said. 'We won't do much—just beat him to pulp. Nobody will know. He'll never trouble you again.'

My heart rate must have touched a hundred and twenty a minute. I could barely register what he was saying.

'But,' he continued, 'there's a price.' He paused, rubbed the discarded cigarette stub with his toe, and lit another. 'You must help us pass all the exams. You must sit in front of us and ... er ... lend us all your answer sheets.'

'That's cheating,' I exclaimed before I could prevent myself.

The compulsive laughers laughed yet again. 'Of course, mate! Do you think you can hire our services for nothing?'

I was breathing normally once again now. Somehow, for some reason, the thought of Ankit Dave being beaten to pulp thrilled my veins. There could be nothing better than to see that miserable pest being squashed flat by these road rollers. The thought of his piercing puppy yelps as he went down was fabulous. I don't know why but the fantasy seemed to calm the restlessness that had been wreaking mayhem in my system ever since our results. I knew the Terrible Trio meant everything they said. They were boys who roamed the school corridors with bicycle chains and kitchen knives carefully concealed from the teachers' eyes. I just had to give a faint nod, and it would be done.

'No, thank you,' I heard myself say firmly. 'I can manage my problems myself.'

More laughter followed catcalls. I stumbled out of the corridor, uncertain where my wobbly knees were leading me. This was my first brush against the villainous trio. I don't know why I had a horrifying feeling that it would not be my last. But I had got away, unscathed. Of all the things my father had warned me against in school, bad company was the cardinal evil. I had almost yielded to the temptation offered by the true descendents of the supreme ruler of hell. What had I been thinking? From an unsteady hobble, I broke into a fearful run, and did not halt until I had reached the familiar walls of my noisy classroom.

May 9, 1994

I was pleased with myself. Mighty pleased. We were the senior-most students in school now. I had reclaimed my old numero uno position. My working physics models had made it to the national level thrice in consecutive years. Mrs Rana, our physics teacher, was probably grinning even in her sleep. Ankit and Rashmi had now been 'going around' for about two years, still canoodling in deserted corners. The Terrible Trio still bumped into me once in a while in empty corridors. They greeted me with their familiar whistles and catcalls, repeating their offer with meaningful winks. I ignored them. Things were going splendidly for me. I knew I had all the fundamental prerequisites for the head boy's position this year. With so much to my credit already, even the vice chancellor could not deny me my right. And so I sat smugly in Mrs Rana's physics class all week.

Ankit Dave was declared the new head boy of the school during the school assembly on Monday. It was the democratic system, the bane of Indian society, that did it. The rest of the student fleet was responsible for my dismal battering. A last-minute secret ballot had been carried out. Thanks to egalitarianism, I had lost by more than a gaping margin. Apparently, there were several charges against Uday Joshi.

'He's too arrogant ...'

'Insensitive ...'

'Wild bouts of rage ...'

'Erratic ...'

'Overbearing ...'

'Arrogant!'

'Aggressive ...'

Rubbish!

'You don't just need to be a good academician, Uday,' said Mrs Rana, sighing. 'For the head boy's post, you need—something more. You need to go an extra mile.'

Etcetera, etcetera, etcetera.

With his new-found confidence ever since he was smitten by the love microbe, Ankit Dave had suddenly acquired all the essential etceteras as well. Now that half of the junior wing was fawning over him, and the opposite gender was swooning over his taller and slimmer latest revised edition, his position was very well consolidated. I despised him for it. With every word of congratulations he received, a fresh gash appeared in my heart. Everything I had achieved had come to zilch. All my hard work, all my gruelling efforts, had been smashed to smithereens thanks to this little pest of a guy.

There was hope yet. The principal had recently made a fresh announcement. Our school had a new patron who was willing to sponsor one student to a university in the United States every year. After class twelve, depending on the unanimous choice of the teachers, one lucky bastard would bid India goodbye. The selection would be based entirely on merit, he said. This one *had to be mine*! There were two contestants for the prize anyway—me and Mr Popular Pest! I couldn't afford to pause for breath.

'Don't worry, son, this will be your moment,' Mr Datta told me kindly. 'You've got a whole chain of awards to your name.'

'You'll get admission in any US university with your record, Uday,' said Mrs Rana. 'Even if this doesn't happen, you could still win a scholarship and go. A student like you doesn't need sponsors! Harvard, Oxford ... they'll welcome you with open arms.'

It was a mystery when and how in the course of the last two years Ankit had managed to slough off his timidity and diffidence. It was miraculous what that non-scientific dame had done to him.

But I believed in my destiny. I pampered my pride. Destiny, as people say, moves in bizarre ways. A few months after Ankit Dave donned the cloak of head boy, he still took care of his responsibilities very sincerely. Bunking classes, that too at school-level, and that too by the senior-most students of the school, was unimaginable. It was a criminal offence, inviting severe penalty. And Mr Popular Pest had begun to crouch behind random walls trying to catch such offenders. It was a grave blunder to trap the Terrible Trio in his net, and confront them with their crime. The compulsive laughers laughed heartily at his moral sermon.

And then the tables turned. Ankit Dave disappeared mysteriously from the scene for a short, tense period. By sheer accident, I caught the Terrible Trio beating my rival ruthlessly to pulp not too far from the boundaries of the school, unobserved. His excruciating puppy yelps that should have been a balm to my soul, made me writhe guiltily instead. They were frightening, hair-raising cries of pain I heard, and I stood there paralysed with sheer terror.

Gautam noticed me first. The merciless kicking abruptly ceased as the other two too turned around to face me. My body went numb when Gautam slowly began to walk towards me. His heavy steps seemed to trample the ground beneath him. He stood at a distance of fifteen centimetres from me, staring unblinkingly into my terror-stricken eyeballs.

'You've seen nothing,' he said softly. 'Nothing, remember. Not a word to anyone, or… '

'Don't worry,' I gasped, without a thought. 'I shan't tell anyone.'

The giant stepped back. He smiled his yellow, toothy smile. *Step one of fraternity initiation.*

It did not trouble my conscience that Ankit Dave stayed away from school for two months, battling for his life first in hospital, then at home. He never revealed the names of his tormentors. Only the probing eyes of his valentine met mine once in a while during his absence. It was as though they were intuitively conscious of the skeletons hanging in my cupboard. But cowardice was greater than shame. I kept my mouth zipped.

I chose my destiny when I decided to keep my guilty lips sealed. It was easy. My parents were apprehensive. I was spending more time on the syllabi of the competitive entrance exams than on my immediate concern—the CSBE boards. But I was blasé. I knew what I was doing.

School exams came and went; the medical and engineering entrance exams came and went. I was still working like a man possessed, determined to win the sponsorship at any cost. There could be no hurdles this time. Mr Popular Pest had been pushed out of the race almost completely midway through the year. There were no more serious adversaries left. I had to be the teachers' choice by default. And once again, when the unanimous choice was announced, the news left me dumbfounded. Ankit Dave beat me again. It was unfathomable. No amount of explanation was good enough. It was impossible. Impossible! Mr Datta himself could barely meet my eyes.

'I don't know how it happened, Uday,' he said. 'The principal went against my recommendation. As the HOD, I did recommend your name, but there must have been a divided house, I guess.'

'Never mind, son,' said Mrs Rana. 'We need people like you in our country. I'm sure you'll make it to IIT. Just opt to stay in Delhi ...'

November 9, 1995

My hazy eyes inspected the list from top to bottom and vice versa for the seventh time—and again. Why couldn't I focus my eyes properly today? I was carefully stringing the printed letters together to read each name twice like a class-one child. This was not possible. This was the last list of the final engineering college entrance exam results. My name figured nowhere. Nowhere at all. I had begun scanning all the lists from the top every time. But my name had eluded me each time. Following my boards, I had whirled through a deluge of such exams, without a break. Where my name should have shone in the top row on every list, it hadn't featured even once—not in the top row, not in the middle, not at the bottom. And today was my last chance. With an appalling seventy-five per cent aggregate in the boards, I could not even hope to enter the precincts of a respectable college if I wanted to do graduation instead. Even in my most harrowing nightmares I had never imagined such a hopeless situation. Me—Uday Joshi, the top-scorer of my school for a decade, the celebrated science wizard, the envy of every student, driven to a wretched cul-de-sac!

Time and destiny had colluded to destroy Uday Joshi. My world was disintegrating. And I had no means to save it. The fantastic skyscraper of my accomplishments seemed to be collapsing faster than the WTO buildings, and I stood there, voiceless, mindless, watching it crumble. I was overwhelmed by shame. Familiar hopeful faces materialised in my mind—of Mr Datta, Mrs Rana, Mr Javed, my own parents, my classmates. The sheer thought of facing any of them now turned my knee joints to detergent powder.

It was sundown. I was still sitting in front of the treacherous list of selected candidates. I was unsure about when I should move or where I should go. Heading home was impossible. Mindlessly, I got up and began to walk down an unfrequented, isolated road, kicking little stones and pebbles on the way. A potpourri of chaotic emotions wrung my soul. I felt an inexplicable wrath begin to boil inside. My feet began to work faster and faster. Bigger and chunkier pebbles went flying from my angry shoes. In my frenzy I failed to notice that one such pebble had landed upon an unfortunate little farmer standing on the roadside. I was too preoccupied with my own troubles. All of a sudden a rough, sun-burnt hand rudely poked me from behind.

'Just what the hell do you think you're doing, old man?' I screamed, turning back to face him.

The enraged farmer's face let out a torrent of abuses. He did not bother to explain the reason behind the instigation, however. The events of the day had left me too weary. Reason was an object from outer space at this time. Without opening my mouth to make an effort at conversation, I paid the man back for his impertinence; that too, with a bonus. I landed a blow at his chest with my sandstone fist.

He faltered and fell, unprepared for the retaliation. But the bugle had been sounded, and the scuffle began. The little man got up and hit me back. The scuffle soon transformed into a more violent brawl. I found myself hitting out not at an unknown farmer face, but at Ankit Dave, at a million more treacherous faces, at my deceitful destiny, at the unseen conspirators who had robbed me of my contented world; and at an unfair and sadistic god. With the appearance of each face, the reckless blows came harder and harder. My weak antagonist cowered and fell again. But I did not—could not—stop. On and on the pounding continued. My ears were too sore to register his agonised cries; eyes, too clouded to notice the blood dangerously spewing out from his multiple wounds. I carried on and on in a maniacal frenzy, finally hitting his head with a huge boulder lying nearby—until I was left with nothing except a spent madness, and a motionless body lying in front of me.

I stood back, gulping oxygen from the air—shell shocked. The realisation of what I had just done began to crawl in. Some semblance of sanity returned. It rattled my nerves. I stared at the body lying before me, wreathed in tiny puddles of blood. It made me nauseous. I looked left and right, forwards and backwards. There wasn't a soul on the road. No living being had witnessed my black deed—nobody—except the wretched occupants of that familiar flashy sedan parked unobtrusively at the narrow turn on the road ahead. Each member of the Terrible Trio looked out of the vehicle—at me. I found beads of sweat slide down my forehead. The trio did not step out. Instead, I saw the car reverse and stop next to me.

'Get in,' uttered an incorporeal voice. I numbly obeyed.

'That … that man—'

'Leave him alone,' said someone gruffly.

They stared at my quivering body, smiling their usual yellow, toothy smiles. We stopped at a lonely roadside ditch almost four kilometres away. They supported me out of the car. I vomited into the dirty hole. They helped me climb back into the car and gave me sweet, rubbery gum to chew.

'Welcome to the club, science wizard,' said Gautam, grinning complacently.

I stared back him vacantly. *Step two of fraternity initiation.*

The bloodied farmer face returned to haunt me in the following weeks and months. Each ding of the doorbell, each screech of the telephone was a white shark's open jaw. It threatened to swallow me whole. At every corner I saw policemen in khaki uniforms walking towards me with ominous handcuffs. I was turning into a virtual paranoiac. Every voice, familiar or unfamiliar, was beginning to startle and terrify. I sought the obituary of the old man, week after week, rummaging through every newspaper. I expected the dead man's relatives begging the public to bring the perpetrator to justice. I saw my revolting face ogle back at me mockingly from the columns of *India's Most Wanted* in my nightmares every night. I was simply waiting to be led to the scaffold. Uday Joshi, the brilliant student, the self-righteous blue eyed boy of the faculty, was a violent psychopath, a criminal, and a murderer.

Nothing happened. The episode shook nothing except my life. My feet never led me down that road again. That road had been a silent witness to my dark deed. I never travelled it again, though I would have simply been an ordinary man walking down an ordinary road.

May 8, 1996

I had now been a virtual member of the Terrible Trio for about six months. Honestly speaking, it wasn't too bad. I liked to believe I was part of the corridors of power, no matter how inadequate a constituent. It meant something. It was still a Terrible Trio. Karan had been absorbed into his father's business immediately after school, and hardly made an appearance now. I made a pathetic surrogate, no doubt, but I did not have an alternative. Neither did they. As long as our leader was happy, the world was still a bearable place. In one of his better moods, Gautam (or Goldy) had mentioned that his father had enough clout in important circles. If Goldy insisted, he might just be willing to turn his generosity towards me.

'He might sponsor you to the US,' he said smiling, imitating the flight of an aeroplane with his right hand.

'Really?' I asked. There suddenly appeared a ray of light in my bleak world.

'Yup,' he said, checking his new Seiko watch. 'But you'll have to wait until next year. This is an important year for him. If the deals go as planned, we'll be richer by a few million next year.'

'Wow!' I said, upping my antennae after a long time.

I had repeated last year's process like an android this year. I had mechanically stepped in and out of the whirlpool of entrance exams. I had dutifully visited several school buildings to check the results. But last year's Uday Joshi was another person. He was a strong-willed, uncompromising student, determined to define his own destiny. He was confident of making his own path in a competitive world. This was an alien soul in my body now—a far cry from the person I once knew as myself. I did not recognise myself any longer. I was a daemon in a cherub's clothing; an impostor. Gone was that brilliant spark that used to be my identity. In the evil tunnel I had inadvertently stumbled into last year, there was no place for the original Uday.

'I'll speak to him,' said Goldy, getting up with a bored yawn. 'But you must wait until next year.'

'I'll wait,' I said quietly. 'I'll wait.'

I was willing to wait. All of a sudden, an importunate desire to leave my ugly world—my sinister past—behind me, resurfaced. I was desperate to run away. It was a delicious thought—walking into ordinary sunshine in a foreign land a million miles away. If this worked, I could still erase the memory of my eventful past; I could still redraft my destiny. Nothing in the world is final except death. And I wasn't dead yet. So, while I waited I registered for some wooly, intellect-insulting course in a lesser college in some remote corner of the city. It neither noticed nor cared about the absence of my repulsive face all through the year.

I conveyed the happy news to my father. 'Gautam's father is willing to sponsor me next year, dad. I'll be going to the US next year.'

Father was happy. 'But be careful, son,' he warned me. 'Why take somebody's obligation when you can achieve it on your own merit? Try to win a scholarship this year. There isn't time.'

I agreed with my father. There wasn't time. Father had suffered a stroke. I had no finances. And therefore, shortcuts were imperative. Last year's Uday could have achieved what his father wanted him to achieve. I had suddenly grown forty years older, and had neither the inclination, nor the energy to persevere my old dreams with the same zest. Goldy's world was promising. If I kept a blind eye towards uncomfortable questions, I could accept his offer easily.

'Come, we'll celebrate Uday's success!' said Goldy, nudging Raghu to stand up.

'What?' I said, wondering what he was getting at now. 'What do you want to do?'

'Oh, just go for a spree,' he said, nudging me too. I obediently stood up. 'I'll show you dad's latest SUV. Come!'

Gautam flew cars, he didn't drive them. He lived up to his reputation, of course. We flew over the speed limit at a hundred and forty miles an hour. We dangerously squeezed through whizzing cars, brushing past heavy traffic vehicles, barely avoiding head-on collisions. We just about managed not to crash down single-lane bridges and misleading flyovers. Ghaziabad zipped past, Hapur and Pilakhwa zoomed. Gajraula and Moradabad were a stomach-churning blur. We were on a high, all of us, squealing, hooting, and screaming wildly. We were oblivious to the panic-stricken public and pedestrians we sent dashing like chickens to dodge our crazy vehicle. It was a mind-boggling, exhilarating experience that momentarily wiped out all unhappy thoughts from my mind.

A kilometre away from Moradabad, on our way back, Goldy knocked that man down. He wasn't speeding. In fact, the engine was hiccupping disgustingly upon the bumpy trail. Before he knew it, he had knocked that man down. Hardly a man though. That boy couldn't have been more than thirteen or fourteen. He wasn't seriously hurt. A few scratches and bruises, that's all. All the hawkers, vendors, and villagers in the vicinity immediately rushed to the site. Indignation dripped from their angry faces. Some stood with wooden staffs in hand. I felt my body temperature drop, and the familiar convulsions returned to torment my body. Goldy and Raghu maintained their cool. They raised no objections to being taken to a nearby police thana. The mention of police turned my heart to tissue paper. We spent the night in the lock-up. For me, it was the roughest ordeal of my life, a terror-soaked darkness I can never forget. It spelt the end for me—the dreaded *suryast* I had been evading all these months. It was over. I was exposed. I believed they would conduct an enquiry. Everything would be discovered. Uday Joshi was trapped.

They released us the next morning without much ado. Only an insignificant amount as recompense was doled out, and we were free. My father thought I had spent the night toiling for Goldy's father. He thought I'd been earning my sponsorship to the United States. He was happy. I never felt more rotten. But I had set off the Uranium 235 chain reaction myself the day I stepped into that evil tunnel, the day I silently stepped into Goldy's sparkling car, burying my black deed in the gutter. I did not know how and where the reaction would end. I only knew that there was bound to be that inevitable explosion in the end.

I became a depraved Faustus who had sold his soul to a wily Mephistopheles. In exchange, I was offered the promise of reincarnation on foreign soil. I played Hide-and-Seek with myself in the dark dungeons of smoke and psychedelia; in grotesque, hard-hitting, memory-smashing parodies of music and dance; in the clutches of *afeem*, *charas*, *ganja*, and other ruthless assassins. Gautam insisted these killer drugs were 'cool'. One needed to get high once in a while. 'Once,' he said, persuasively. 'Just this once. Nothing will happen.'

I obliged ... usually. It would not have been wise to antagonise my patron. Liquor came easy for the liquor mogul, and we became its committed servants. It was a euphoric experience to lose ourselves thus—to live in the moment, for the moment, burying all other disquieting memories underground. It was easy to allow the incubus world to suck our souls. So far I had only heard such stories, or watched them on TV. Now it was for real. One night we found ourselves amongst warm female bodies exhibiting their pleasing chattels to our eyes. We surrendered to the craving of our ravenous loins. At eighteen, I was no longer a virgin, and I loved it.

September 14, 1996

I stared blankly at page number one hundred and thirty two of my physics book, chewing the ragged stub of my pencil absent-mindedly. For the hundred and thirty second time I wondered why things had gone awry for me. Future had seemed so promising, so certain, when I was younger.

'I don't know how it happened,' I said aloud, suddenly remembering the school sponsorship that had slipped through my fingers like dry salt.

'It was Mr Datta's doing,' responded Raghu simply, after a moment's pause. 'Our respected Datta sir!'

I stared at him, and then at Goldy, who nodded his massive head in agreement.

'Mr Datta? How?' I asked, stupefied. 'He was my champion till the end … right from class six!'

Goldy sniggered. 'How naïve can you be, Mr Science Wizard! Nobody could have beaten you to it with your record, you know that. Everybody knew that. But it required the HOD's final approval, and the HOD gave a nod to you know who.'

He downed his drink. 'Why? Simple. He needed a favour from our puny scalawag's oh-so-important daddy, haha! How is it that his sister's daughter got married to Mr Dave's elder son just ten days after junior Mr Dave left for the US? Couldn't dare to sacrifice Ankit Dave for you, could he?'

'But—'

'But what?' said Raghu, prepared to counter any argument.

The duo's words wiped the vapour off my brain. Suddenly, I could see everything perfectly. The confusion cleared, exposing Mr Debojit Datta's clever designs. Mr Debojit Datta had just given me an agonising punch in the solar plexus. How innocently I had believed him all these years.

Goldy stared at me, licking his upper lip. 'Pay back time for Datta sir, ain't it?'

I took a deep breath. Familiar faces materialised in my mind once again—of my teachers, parents, classmates, friends. Why didn't they prick my conscience now? Why did they arouse only rage? *How could they allow Mr Debojit Datta to get away*?

I didn't feel guilt pangs any more.

'What do you have in mind?' I asked him. *The fraternity initiation process was complete.*

It was twelve midnight. The physics book was carelessly snapped shut as the Terrible Trio's round table conference began in earnest.

September 19, 1996

Piyali Datta was twenty years old, a student of third year BA History hons at a renowned college in the university campus. She had a pleasant face and pleasant features. She was a pleasant person. Every morning she jogged two kilometres around a small local park. She walked further two kilometres to college upon returning, and repeated the practice in the evening. She seldom caught a bus. Buses were overcrowded, about-to-burst, groaning monsters on the road anyway. Her daily timetable made the task convenient for us.

It was strangely a chilly night for September. The low buzzing of nocturnal insects sounded sinister in the silence. In the cold isolation of that wilderness, those ghastly, tragic screams began, and continued unmitigated, curdling my blood. But there was no one around for miles. We had made sure of that. She could scream all she wanted.

Goldy's gorilla body was moving frenziedly upon her naked torso fastened to the ground. He was clawing her injured limbs, ruthlessly pushing his member between her quivering thighs—a gruesome display. He was ripping her as though stimulated by her horrific cries. My sleepy eyes witnessed his hysterical love making with perfect calm. Apathy had spread into my body and soul like a malignant tumour. I watched his performance impassively, standing against the trunk of a hunched tree. The throbbing continued as his giant body melted into Raghu's leaner, taller frame, repeating the act. He disregarded the nauseating blood stains tainting the earth. And slowly Raghu's body melted in front of my unfocused eyes, and he was me and I was him, and I was groping the dark valley of her unconscious, submissive body, moving feverishly—slaughtering her dignity with sadistic appetite. I was hitting out wildly at her traitor father, hitting out at my own naivety.

Perhaps I should have felt some regret when I woke up the next morning. Perhaps, in a clearer head dispossessed of drugs, some semblance of shame and sorrow should have crept in. But these had become alien vocabulary now. I had tossed my conscience into a shredder and never turned to look back. I had dumped my remorse into a toilet bowl and flushed it down the drain. By this time, only venomous thoughts flowed from my heart like dirty water from a drainpipe. There was a certain sense of contentment in my veins that morning now that the long-overdue revenge had been taken. Mr Datta should not have thrown the gauntlet towards me so recklessly.

The news appeared in a small column under 'city news' in every newspaper four days later. Mr Datta's young daughter had been found hanging from the ceiling fan in her bedroom—the standard solution for most rape victims in our wonderful country. She had used her dupatta to take her life. There was nothing illuminating in the suicide note except that she had cried rape. She could not identify her assailants. It was dark, and she recognised none of the three. Some from the general public suspected Gautam Sahni and his Terrible Trio behind the criminal act. Though there were several hushed whispers rippling in the city, nobody could openly confront him with the charge, for lack of evidence. I wasn't scared now. This was justice. We continued to roam the roads, vicious and violent, and still at large.

January 8, 1997

I had known Prem Singh from childhood. He was a gardener in our locality. Sometime in the past he had done a short stint in our house. He was quiet and efficient. He had a sagacious face, and slightly stooping shoulders. His wife brought *jaamun*s for us every season. He used to climb the *jaamun* trees and shake the loaded branches hard so that the juicy little purple balls broke free and fell upon the ground. She gathered the best ones in her aanchal, not bothering about the permanent stains they left behind on her dress. Prem Singh used to bring us the best *jaamun*s every year ... just as he brought us the best *shehtoot*s, and the best *singhada*s. God alone knows where he found the most delectable fruits.

And there he was, standing at our door, his eyes brimming. His wife and three little girls followed timidly behind. His right arm was lying limp, and he could barely manage to hold his coat with his left. My mother was engaged in an animated conversation with him. I heard his despondent account, sitting in the next room. His right arm had become paralysed. On New Year's Eve, some crazy party animals had left a local club past midnight, choked with alcohol. They had set themselves wild on the road in a black Tata Safari, completely oblivious to their bad-tempered vehicle's antics. The directionless vehicle had slapped his arm as it brusquely brushed past him. Thankfully, he had survived, but his right arm had been badly damaged.

Of course I knew the story. I knew the vehicle. I knew what had happened. I was in the wretched vehicle when the incident occurred! Only, I did not know it was Prem Singh we had injured. We were too drunk, all of us. And, as usual, Goldy just revved up the engine and the plane took off. We never realised how high we had soared until there was that unforeseen bird hit, and Goldy slammed on the brakes. I could only make out an injured figure lying doubled up near the footpath, whimpering. We did not stop as the crowd started gathering around him. Goldy did not stop. He simply reversed and pushed the accelerator as far as it would go.

'Hey! What are you doing?' I asked, surprised.

'Nothing,' replied Gautam casually. 'Just knocked down a foolish fellow, that's all. His arm's injured, I guess.'

'Aren't we stopping?' I enquired uncertainly.

'No!' Gautam snapped back at me. 'You know what happened the last time we stopped. That man's alive. Nothing's happened. If we stop, the crowd will only pester us and make us shell out more money. No point. They'll take care of him.'

And we did not stop. It was common knowledge that Gautam's gang was behind this episode. The people did not know that I formed a part of his squad. In the dead of the night, through the tinted-glass windows of the automobile, nobody saw or identified my culpable face. Our public knew there were three members in his gang. They assumed that the third was Karan Bajaj. I was only a ghost actor, an invisible perpetrator nobody ever saw or suspected ... just as I had been when the Piyali Datta episode occurred; just as I had been all these months—leading a Jekyll and Hyde life. The fact was unknown to any soul, including my own family. I was an infrequent visitor to the Sahni residence, and an unremarkable, wallpaper-like presence when I was. Nobody associated Uday Joshi with the likes of Gautam Sahni. Nobody could. Though the world knew Gautam was behind the incident, not one person had the courage to stand up against the offender; not one person was willing to testify against him in court. Prem Singh's depressing affair left me somewhat shaken. How much lower could I stoop?

July 20, 1997

Gautam was sweating—literally. Plump little drops of oily liquid doused his hairy face, and neck, and chest, and arms. He was taking deep breaths, as though to calm himself. Raghu and I waited silently till he could muster enough strength to speak.

'I need dough,' he declared. Neither Raghu nor I spoke.

'I need dough,' he repeated, rather urgently.

'Dough for what?' said Raghu. 'Ask uncle ...'

'No!' he cried. 'I can't ask him for money. He ... he doesn't know I do drugs!'

'Oh.'

'That peddler,' he explained, still sweating profusely. 'My dependable supplier ... he's been asking me for money for all those cartons I bought from him five months ago.'

I stared at him. While I had managed to limit myself to the allures of the not-so-lethal drugs, Goldy seemed to have given himself over to them completely. Even Raghu had directed his energies towards our more reckless and violent acts, but steered clear of this suicidal habit. Neither of us had any money. I, being from a middle class family, had never had much anyway. And ever since my father had suffered a stroke, I was even worse off. Our only source of income was my mother's paltry school teacher's salary, and my intermittent tutorial jobs. I had latched on to Gautam Sahni precisely in the hope of making some quick cash myself. I hadn't seen a phantom of a windfall yet; rather the reverse, with a host of auxiliary problems. I certainly had no surpluses. Raghu, though from an affluent enough family, had neither parent compassionate enough to oblige him. The best they could do was leave him alone to manage his own affairs, while they battled their own polite-society issues. If he wanted money, he could very well earn it.

It was a unanimous decision to resort to kidnapping. My worthy collaborators knew the ropes. It was easy. Goldy even had an ideal hideout in mind, ready and waiting for our victim's warehousing. Goldy and Raghu abducted eight-year-old Piyush, grandson of business tycoon, Ram Chawla. They got him easily from the back gate of the school after school hours. He was dragged roughly into a white Maruti van. They arrived in Muzaffar Nagar following a monotonous expedition, switching number plates, and switching vehicles. They did not meet any uncomfortable glitches on the way. In the meanwhile, I prepared the derelict house for their welcome all by myself in the foreign city.

We had decided upon an amount of three lakh rupees as ransom. A desperate Goldy demanded five. We kept Piyush sedated, of course. Raghu's resourcefulness came in useful here. The distraught family eventually agreed to our demands, but the negotiations carried on for a week. Each time Goldy called, we dreaded an instantaneous police raid. One day, Raghu and I returned to the house after buying our usual supplies, and found a flustered Goldy sweating on the couch, palpitating.

'What happened?' asked Raghu, sounding genuinely concerned.

Gautam looked at us, the whites of his eyes suddenly a bloody red. 'I shot him,' he said.

'What!' We were shocked.

'I shot him dead with my pistol,' Gautam said again, staring stupidly at the weapon.

'Gautam, how could you!' I bellowed. 'He was only eight years old! And we were getting the ransom, you FOOL!'

'He was awake,' said Goldy, retaliating. 'He was awake and screaming like a hyena. The idiot would have woken up the whole neighbourhood!'

'And so you shot him *dead*?' Raghu was as dazed as I was. The zero degree Celsius feeling had begun to descend upon us.

'Yeah,' Gautam replied, sliding down to the ground.

He had already slid down to the bottom of hell. His conscience smelt of rancid cheese. But—who was I to pass any judgement? Trapped in this situation, we were hardly left with any options. We silently wrapped the body in a khaki green hold-all, and loaded it in the car. We dumped it in a deserted trench in Khatauli. Yet, I had a pesky feeling that this time we could not escape untouched.

I was right. I don't know how they discovered the body. The police traced Gautam Sahni, thanks to Mr Sahni's derelict property in Muzaffar Nagar. He got a tip-off though. His father's faithful minions did that much for him. Panting, sweating, he issued us a warning. If he drowned, he would not drown alone, he said. He was determined to take us down with him. His father arranged for his flight from the country. Goldy didn't make it. Somehow, I knew he wouldn't. He met his nemesis on the way to the airport, soaring as usual in his flashy SUV. There was a macabre head-on collision with a truck. His body was so hideously charred that they couldn't even locate the scattered bits.

Raghu vanished mysteriously from the city after this episode. Perhaps he got himself a new identity. I neither saw nor heard of him again. With their prime offender and witness dead, the police couldn't trace any others. They didn't know how many there had been. I returned home to my parents. I had to supply them with a vague reason for opting out of Goldy's father's company. I also had to invent a reason for declining his offer for a sponsorship. Goldy's father still seemed unaware of my role in his son's life. As everybody else, he too believed that Gautam's triumvirate comprised his son, Raghu, and Karan. He had never cared to acquaint himself with further details. I was still an insubstantial phantasm, a vampire gliding in and out of people's lives, unseen and unsuspected.

I qualified for a post-graduation in Microbiology at a famed university in the United States. Simultaneously, I received an offer from a relatively obscure university in Frankfurt. I had won scholarships to both. I opted for Germany.

I spent ten years abroad, shuttling between different countries and time zones. I authored noteworthy papers, won awards, and attended international seminars and lectures. I almost reclaimed the life I had once lived. Almost. Climbing each rung of the ladder, I distanced myself further from my other, sinister self. But, I am not free. My fugitive spirit lives in constant fear. All perfumes of France will not sweeten these guilty hands.

Even today, those horrifying memories return to haunt me in my slumber. After countless yoga sessions and art-of-living classes with the most eminent gurus, those grisly recollections still remain like obdurate pencil impressions left by an untidy eraser. At times, the burden increases hundredfold. It pounds me under its weight—when I have to face people like you, my friends—ordinary people from the ordinary world, and answer their ordinary questions. Social networking sites are but such hellholes. My cotton wool soul cannot bear the burden any longer. Ordinariness is extraordinary to a senseless, shrivelled soul like mine. I walk on this earth like an exhumed corpse—seeking, sweating, seeking… aching for that illusory sweetness called ordinariness, and the bliss of anonymity.

Acknowledgements

A big Thank You! to Jaya mashi and Adam Corson-Finnerty, who took the trouble of plodding through my very first (and badly overwritten) draft of the book, and prodded me to do several more, till the manuscript finally found some shape; to Sanju and Pinku—ordinarily non-readers, for succeeding in reading all the stories, and offering their comments and encouragement; to my mom for her candid feedback, and for helping me with my Bengali dialogues; to my friends, Hema and Bindiya, for always being there; and to Monica Arora, my friend and editor, for all her contributions to the book.

And, oh, a big Thank you! to Trixie, for being a steadfast companion throughout, and for allowing me to whack the rusks from her tin, without which I may not have survived the long hours at the comp!

ALSO AVAILABLE FROM GYAANA BOOKS

Of Wooing, Woes, & Wanderings

Amitabha Chatterjee

Rs 250 $ 8.95 £ 6.99

Rajarshi can barely stammer a few words in Spanish. Marisel does not know a word of English. He is a young, inexperienced Indian with the baggage of Indian values in tow. She is an expressive Venezuelan, bold and open in her ways. They meet in El Tigre, at a surprise party thrown by Rajarshi's friends, Alan and Pedro, to welcome him to his new job at the oil rig. The gathering is also meant to announce his arrival to any interested Latino women.

A few days later, Rajarshi is surprised to find the lady waiting for him outside his villa. And hence begins Rajarshi's humorous saga, across countries and cultures, as his job takes him from one oil rig to another.

Of Wooing Woes, and Wanderings is entertaining, fluid, and sensitive. Chatterjee explores the love-life and profession of an Indian oilman in the bleakness of oil rigs in the world, a little-explored theme so far.

'Hello, Vishal?' she said.

Immediately, I knew it was her. Back from the past to haunt me.

When Detective Vishal Bajaj receives a call from his old flame, Aditi, on a Sunday afternoon, he is staggered by the resurgence of buried emotions. Aditi married Sunil three years ago. Now, Sunil's elder brother, Anil, has been found murdered at their farmhouse, and the first person Aditi turns to for help is Vishal.

Vishal sets out to solve the mystery with his hopeless but faithful sidekick, Pranay; and Inspector Babu, a pompous and limelight-loving policeman, for company.

A delightful page-turner, Katyal's novel will keep you riveted and grinning till the end.